CHASING THE LIGHT

CHASING THE LIGHT

JOEL S. ZARLEY

PURPLE PALM MEDIA

COLUMBUS, OHIO MMX

To my parents, Ted and Isabelle Zarley

רוֹאִיהָיו ;רוֹאִיהְי, סיהֹלֶאְרֶמאֹיו

from the Hebrew

dixitque Deus fiat lux et facta est lux

from the Latin

και είπε ο Θεός γενηθήτω φως και εγένετο φως

from the Greek

And said God let there be light, and there was light.

from the English

Chapter One

BERLIN, GERMANY-January, 1945

The pounding became louder as he slowly eased into consciousness, and his dream faded into reality. One moment he was standing with his father at the Neue Pinakothek staring at *Village Street* by Franz von Lenbach, and the next he was jolted into reality by the coldness of the night air and the hardness of his cot.

He loved when he dreamt about his father, and the art that he taught young Rudolph to love. He and his father would spend hours in the Neue Pinakothek and the other prominent museums of Munich in the 1920s, and by far his favorite painting was *Village Street*. He loved the serenity and quiet of the muted colors, and the implied strength of the lone standing man. He never really knew where the "village" was supposed to be, but he always believed it was in America. (Of course, it could have just been the cowboy hat which the man wore.) His father helped him ponder such things, and made him realize that there was much beauty in the world to discover.

Rudolph Zeffner sat upright, listening to the unyielding pounding that seemed to be coming from the front door of the museum. Of course, "museum" was a far too generous term for the sparse building which he currently occupied.

For now it was only some store rooms, an office area, and small space that did multiple duty as Zeffner's kitchen, bedroom, and living area. But soon, the works he collected and cataloged here would become part of the greatest museum the world had ever known, for he was helping to build the Führermuseum.

The Führermuseum was the brainchild of Adolph Hitler himself, and would encompass the world's greatest collection of art, in the greatest museum the world had ever known. It was to be built in Linz, Austria—the birthplace of the Führer.

Of course, Rudolph Zeffner was not the only German art expert to be toiling to build the Führermuseum. He was one of many working out of similar workshops across Germany and many foreign cities that had fallen to the Reich. However, Zeffner's territory was Berlin—the capital of the Third Reich. Perhaps the only more prestigious assignment would have been Paris itself.

Zeffner was only in his twenties, but he was already considered an expert in the history and value of art by those who followed such things. His personal area of expertise was historical religious art, but really all methods and genres interested him. He had been personally recruited to this post by Dr. Hans Posse. Posse had been named *Sonderbeauftragter des Führers*, special emissary to the Führer, and was chosen by Hitler himself to build his museum.

Zeffner rose from his cot and stumbled into the shadows of the flickering candles in his room. It was dark and cold, but it had been that way for so long now Zeffner barely realized it anymore. It would have been clear to anyone with half a brain that the war was not going well for Germany, but anyone with half a brain would also not speak such a thing out loud. The power this time had been out for nearly three weeks—a new record since the basic modern conveniences of life started to break down in Berlin.

But still, Zeffner ignored those thoughts and the suffering he saw around him, and continued to help build the collection. Because, regardless of what happened to Germany and the war, the art would always survive. And in the art there was beauty—and truth. Plus, he still had wood to burn in his stove, so the Fatherland continued to provide.

Zeffner picked the candle up off the small table beside his bed. He cursed himself for dozing off without extinguishing the candle. Wax was at a premium during the war, and he only had a small box of candles left. He desperately needed to conserve them. Otherwise, he would be sitting in darkness by late afternoon.

He walked toward the door where the frantic pounding continued. He quickly pulled open the door, startling the young man standing on the other side.

"Sir," he stammered. "I'm sorry to disturb you so late."

"Yes, Herr Soldier, what can I do for you this late night?" Zeffner asked somewhat hesitantly.

"Sir, are you Herr Zeffner? I have been sent to bring these trinkets to Herr Zeffner of the museum." The young man said, shivering and motioning toward a small canvas bag he had slung over his shoulder.

Zeffner stepped into the open doorway, and as his eyes became more accustomed to the dark night, he took in the vision of the soldier standing in front of him.

He was a soldier only in that he was wearing the uniform of the Reich, but underneath it he could not have been more than a boy of about fifteen. The boy's uniform was threadbare, and he shivered violently.

"Yes, my young friend," Zeffner said, and puffing out his chest. "I am Herr Zeffner of the Führermuseum."

The boy looked relieved, as if the prospects of continuing his search for the man he was sent to find would have been far too daunting to contemplate.

"Oh wonderful, sir," the young soldier said. "May I please leave these trinkets with you? My commander believes they may have some value to the museum. They were confiscated from the *Juden*."

Zeffner cringed when he heard the word. He tried his best to stay ignorant of what was going on around him. Just as he worked to ignore the failing electricity and lack of heat, he tried never to think about what else could be going on. Art was the beauty; art was the truth. And in his mind he could not reconcile that the Fürher who so valued the art he loved, could cause anything so ugly.

"Of course you may," Zeffner said, feeling pity on the shivering boy. "But you must also allow me the pleasure of sharing dinner with a brave soldier of the Fatherland. Please, please come in and join me."

The young soldier looked around nervously, but the pull of the warmth from the room beyond the door was too tempting to resist.

"I guess I could take a few moments to enjoy your hospitality sir. I haven't yet had dinner—or lunch."

Zeffner smiled at the young soldier, and slapped his hand on his shoulder. "Good, good, Herr Soldier. I consider it my honor."

Zeffner guided the soldier through the door and forced it closed against the wailing Winter wind.

After they had eaten a dinner of biscuits, and some roasted rabbit Zeffner had purchased from a local merchant (well, at least Zeffner chose to believe it was rabbit), the soldier reminded Zeffner of the bag he had brought for the museum.

"My commander believes the items may have some value to the museum," the soldier said. "If they do prove to be valuable, he hopes that you will let Herr Posse know that it was Colonel Zeigmand who brought them to the curator's attention."

"Of course, of course," Zeffner said. "I will also let Dr. Posse know of the brave, young soldier who walked them through the snow to bring them to the Fürhermuseum. What is your name Private?"

"Herr Zeffner, I am Adolph Schmidt. I'm proud to share the name of our Führer," the boy said with obvious pride.

Zeffner smiled at the young man. In the right time, under the right circumstances, he was sure that he could spend some pleasant time with this boy. He quickly shook the thought out of his head. This was not the time, nor the place, and in the Reich there was *only one thing* worse than being one of the *Juden*…

"Well, Private Schmidt who shares the name of our Führer," Zeffner said with a wide grin. "Let's see what art treasures you have brought."

Zeffner took the bag and dumped the contents on the table in front of him. He lit a second candle so that he could better view the items.

He quickly sorted through a pile of mismatched jewelry,

a few pieces of china, some small crystal figurines, and a small clear stone resembling a piece of quartz. He held the stone in his hands, and stared at it intently. He wondered if he might still be dreaming—until the sound of the soldier's voice pulled him back to the reality.

"Sir," the soldier asked with audible hope in his voice. "Are these items of any value to the Führer's museum?"

"Well," Zeffner said, doing his best to sound nonchalant. "The crystal figurines may have some minor place in the museum, but the rest is pretty much just Jewish trash. Cheap paste designed to look like real gems."

The young soldier was visibly dejected, and Zeffner quickly realized his disappointment.

"But, Private Schmidt, any contribution to the Führer-museum has value to the German people. Let me write a letter of receipt—and gratitude—that you can present to your commander. And, let him know that Herr Posse will be personally told of his consideration."

A bright smile returned to the young soldier's face.

"And," Zeffner continued. "Let me give you something for your trouble."

Zeffner pulled a pair of gloves and a heavy wool scarf from this dresser drawer, and a few Marks from a tray on his desk.

"These will help keep you warm and fed," he said.

"Oh no, Herr Zeffner, I couldn't accept any more of your kindness," the solder said.

"Of course you can, it is my honor to be kind to one who so bravely serves the Fatherland," he said. Then with a wink he added, "please feel free to come by and personally accept my kindness whenever you wish."

The soldier looked at him with some curiosity, but then quickly broke his gaze.

"Thank you again for bringing these items and your wonderful company," Zeffner said as he led the soldier to the door.

"Heil Hitler," the solder said, giving Zeffner the stiff armed salute of the Third Reich.

"Heil Hitler," Zeffner returned. Then he watched the solder turn and walk off into the cold, dark German night.

Zeffner practically ran to the large bookshelf at the far end of the room, carrying the clear stone brought by the soldier with him. He quickly scaled a ladder beside it to retrieve a large dusty volume from near the top.

It was a Jewish book, so he carefully made sure that it was always hidden. He flipped through the book until he came to the page he was looking for. He stared at the page, and at the stone he held in his hand.

"*Tzohar*," he said in a hushed whisper.

Chapter Two

DORCHESTER, ENGLAND-August, 2005

Adolph Schmidt sat on the front porch of his large farmhouse, and stared across the field facing him. There would be no crops for market this year; no harvest at all to speak of. Over the past several years his farming efforts had been dwindling to less and less, until finally there was nothing.

This year he could not afford to hire any of the migrant workers who shuffle among the farms of Southwest England. His daughters would have gladly given him the money if he would have asked, but he did not do so. In this heart, he knew it was time to stop.

The farm was dying. But, that was OK—he believed he was too. He felt very uneasy and nervous about the morning's visitor who had just left. He was concerned that he had said too much. But, what difference could that make now? These things had happened over half a century ago.

Adolph Schmidt was German by birth, but a British Subject by choice. He had been captured by the Allies during a fierce battle outside of Hanover, just a few days before the British liberated the camp at Bergen-Belsen.

He had never worked within the camps himself, although he had helped prepare the inmates for transportation to the internment centers. Over the years, he had tried to tell himself that he had not really understood what had happened there; that he was too young, and that the information had been kept from him by those he served in the German command. He tried very hard for a very long time to believe that. But, laying in darkness during the quiet nights in the decades that followed after the war, he could never really fully convince himself. It was a pain he had never discussed—not even with Alice.

He had been brought to England as a POW on the eve of his sixteenth birthday. At the time of his arrival, he no longer cared whether he lived or died. He was exhausted, starving, and sick. He felt like an old man even though he was only a teenager.

His British captors had been good to him, all things considered. They had fed him and nursed him back to health. He was grateful everyday that he had been captured by the British and not the Russians. Because he believed the Russians would not only have let him die, they would have tortured him while doing so.

Nearly all of the German POWs who were physically able were put to work in English factories or on farms to help take the place of the British men who had been pulled into the war effort. He was placed into a camp near Dorchester, and was assigned to work on a small local strawberry farm.

The couple who owned the farm were the Brysons—Earnest and Mary. They were in their fifties, and had never been able to have any children of their own. The Brysons had desperately needed help with the farm, although they were at first uncomfortable with the idea of a Nazi prisoner working in their family business. However, soon after his arrival Mary Bryson's maternal instincts kicked in, and young Adolph became like a member of the family.

The war in Europe officially ended in the Summer of 1945, but conflicting with the statutes of the Geneva Convention, England refused to begin repatriating German POWs until well into 1946. The British economy simply could not bear giving up the free labor as it struggled during the post-war rebuilding.

By that point, however, Adolph had no interest in repatriation. Everything he had ever known or loved in Germany was now long gone. He had joined the German army shortly after his parents had been killed as the last refuge of an orphan. But now, in England with the Brysons, he finally felt at home. He finally felt like he was a member of a family again.

When the papers finally came through giving Adolph his "freedom," he was heartbroken. He had grown to love his life on the farm—even referring to Mary Bryson as *Mutti*. A term of endearment which she adored since she had no children of her own to call her *mummy*.

"You don't have to leave us, you know," Earnest Bryson said to him one day after they had received the papers. "We need you here. Your Mutti—*your Mutti and I*—need you here."

"But will the government allow it?" Adolph had asked.

"If they won't, then we'll adopt you."

Of course, adopting an adult former prisoner of war would not have been as simple as Earnest Bryson made it sound. But fortunately, it never had to come to that. With the Bryson's sponsorship, and Adolph's proven willingness to be a productive member of British society, he was granted a work visa and was permitted to stay. Many years later, he gave up his German birthright altogether and became a British citizen.

He met and married a local girl named Alice, and while her family were none too happy about her union with a former Nazi at first, they also came to love Adolph as a member of their family, just as the Brysons had. Over the years, his German accent faded, and Alice frequently teased him about his rapidly developing "East Ender" cadence.

They had two children—both girls, and he was pleased that Brysons were able to enjoy them as their own grand-children before they both passed away. Adolph and Alice had built a cottage on a small plot of land on the strawberry farm, and with the passing of the Brysons, the entire farm and estate was left to Adolph.

Alice had died in 2000 after a long battle with cancer. Several years earlier, both girls had moved away to go to university. Emma was now an investment banker in London, and Abby was a professor of anthropology at an American university in California.

Adolph Schmidt was now all alone on the strawberry farm which had been his home since he was a teenager. While the girls visited him as much as their busy schedules would allow, and called him frequently, it did little to soothe the intense loneliness he felt.

Maybe that was why he so readily agreed to talk to the strangers who had recently been showing up at his door.

It started about a week ago, with a man who called himself Hadar Levensen. He had shown up at the farmhouse one morning, knocking on the door. The interruption had surprised him, since his visitors lately had been few and far between. And, while the visit was unexpected, it was not unappreciated. Adolph had been anxious to talk to anyone— even this Jewish stranger.

Hadar Levensen had explained that he was doing research for an Israeli museum on Jewish art and jewelry which had been confiscated from concentration camp victims during the war. In particular, he was searching for information on a specific gem that had been taken from an old rabbi named Meir Lazarus.

As Hadar Levensen said the name of the rabbi, he stared intently at Adolph's face; looking for some indication of recognition. Adolph felt the man's eyes boring into him, and it gave him a chill. For a moment, his memory of his time in the German army felt as real and raw as it had sixty years ago. He felt that this man hated him, regardless of the pretense of civility as they sat across the table from each other in his dining room.

Adolph said that he had remembered the old rabbi. There had been rumors among the German soldiers and the other inmates that this man was over one hundred years old. However, he said that he had never quite believed the stories.

He was not sure why at the time, but Adolph did not feel comfortable telling this man the story of the night that he took the items confiscated to the Führermuseum. He felt it would be a mistake to tell this Israeli that he knew exactly of the gem of which he spoke. Partially due to his own feelings of guilt over his involvement; partially due to the fact that this man truly frightened him for some reason.

Instead, he told him that he remembered no such item, and that it had probably been taken from the rabbi long before he had arrived at the processing center where Adolph worked.

The Israeli looked as though he did not completely believe Adolph's story, but after a few brief follow-up questions, pressed no further. The man thanked Adolph for his time, and left the farmhouse.

Two days later, the Arabs came to visit him.

Adolph was surprised to receive two visitors in one week, but was especially surprised when he saw who these visitors were. He did not catch (or completely understand) their names. Only one of the men spoke to him, acting as a translator for the other.

They too were asking about the old rabbi named Meir Lazarus, and the gem he had once possessed. This time, Adolph admitted to not only remembering the rabbi, but also saying that he believed he had also seen the gem. However, he told the men, he believed that the gem had been with the rabbi when he had boarded the train for the camp.

When they rose to leave, the man who was not speaking English made a comment to the one who was acting as the translator. The translator stopped, and looked squarely at Adolph.

"We would like to thank you for the work that you performed many years ago," he said.

Adolph felt as though he had been kicked in the stomach. After they left, he sat alone in the dark and cried for the first time since Alice had died.

Then, this morning, the third visitor arrived.

This man was from the American South, and told Adolph his name was Morris Dew. Unlike the first two visitors, this man offered no pretense of "research" or "study" for his queries. He simply introduced himself to Adolph Schmidt, sat down in a chair beside him on the front porch of the old farmhouse, and began asking questions.

"Sir, I would like to know if you remember an old Jew named Meir Lazarus," Dew said in a rolling Southern drawl. "You would have encountered him when he was being prepared for the camps."

A week ago he would have been shocked by the visitor's bluntness and demeanor. Now, however, he took it as just a matter of course.

"Yes, I remember him. He was an elderly rabbi—some said he was over one hundred years old."

"From what I can tell, he might have been one hundred and fifty—or more."

"That's impossible! No one can live to be that old!"

"Anything is possible," Morris Dew said. "When one possesses the *Holy Light*."

Adolph looked at his visitor with wide-eyed surprise.

"And, from the look on your face I know that you know exactly what I'm talking about," Dew said.

Adolph Schmidt did know what this stranger was talking

about. He knew, and he was tired of thinking about it—of dreaming of it. At one time he thought he would never be able to tell another living soul about that night. But now, he was old and tired and he needed to unburden himself. This man was the third visitor this week who was forcing him to remember. Telling his tale may be the only way to free himself of it.

"Yes, I know of what you speak. I saw the light myself, but for many years I convinced myself that I had imagined it."

Morris Dew sat forward on his chair with excitement. In his entire life—in the entire life of his father's church—this was the closest anyone had ever come to the Holy Light. He was talking with someone who had actually seen it.

"You did not imagine anything. Everything you thought you saw—everything you suspected—it is all true. Tell me— *everything.*"

Adolph Schmidt swallowed hard, and began recalling the events of that January night over sixty years ago. It was the first time he had ever spoken it out loud.

"I was ordered by my commanding officer to take a small bag of jewelry and other trinkets confiscated from the *Juden*—" he stopped sharply, and tightly closed his eyes, as if trying to rewind what he had just said. "Taken from the Jewish prisoners before they boarded the train to the camps, to a museum office in Berlin."

"A museum?"

"Well, it was called a museum, but at the time it was little more than old run-down flat. It served as a collections point for the Fürhermuseum. My commander was terrified of being sent to the Russian front, and he believed if he could be credited with making some significant contribution to Hitler's pet project, he might somehow be spared."

"And, was he?"

The slightest of a smile crossed Adolph's lips. "I heard he was killed in a battle with the Russians just a few months later."

"Tell me about the light," the American man said.

"At first I had no idea what was even in the bag that Colonel Zeigmand had given me, and I honestly did not care. I just wanted to complete the assignment and get it over with. It was over a five mile walk to the museum collector, and it was bitterly cold."

The American nodded politely, and leaned in toward the old man—encouraging him to continue.

"I got lost. Hopelessly and utterly lost," Adolph said, his voice barely above a whisper. "Finally, I just gave up. It was freezing, and I was exhausted and starving. I collapsed next to a tree in an empty beet field, and lay there waiting to die. I had always heard that the moments before one froze to death were very pleasant—and I was anxious for the feeling to come to me."

"But, you obviously did not die. What happened?"

"Something in the sack I carried began to glow, and it startled me."

The American sat ever further at the edge of his chair now, barely able to contain his excitement.

"At first, I thought I was hallucinating—a symptom of my rapidly approaching death. But then, I opened the bag and pulled out the glowing stone. I looked deeply into its light, and I began to warm. Not only that, but I began to *feel*."

"Feel? What did you feel?"

"I *felt* every important moment of my life that has happened since then. I felt the moment I met Alice; I felt our wedding day; I felt the first times I held each of my own daughters. I believe I even felt the moment I would die."

"And," Morris Dew said. "What did that feel like?"

"It felt a lot like today."

The American did nothing to acknowledge the old man's final remark, but instead pressed him to continue.

"What happened then?" he asked.

"I pulled myself off the ground, and continued my journey to find the museum collector. Before, I had been completely lost in the cold, dark night, but after that I knew exactly where to go."

"Did you find the museum collector?"

"Yes, I did. And, I gave him the clear stone and the other trinkets. Although, by then, it had long stopped glowing."

"Did you tell him what you had experienced?"

"No, because I still wasn't sure exactly what I had experienced. Besides, by then I was convinced the whole thing might have been an hallucination."

Morris Dew sat facing Adolph Schmidt, his face only a few inches from the old man's. He looked intently into his eyes, and spoke slowly and quietly.

"Tell me to whom you gave the Holy Light. Tell me the museum collector's name."

"His name was Rudolph Zeffner," the old man said, and he slumped hard against the back of his chair. He felt a tear roll down his cheek, and he knew that he had told a horrible secret. A secret that he knew he could never take back.

Milton Dew closed his eyes as if in prayer, and just kept repeating, "thank you, thank you, thank you..." over and over again. At first Adolph thought he was speaking to him, but then realized the American was expressing his thanks to some unseen being not on the porch with them.

They both sat there for a few moments, then Adolph struggled to pull himself from his chair.

"I'm parched from all the talking. I'll make us some tea."

"No, no," Morris Dew said. "Please, let me do it. After all, you have been so helpful to me."

The man raised and entered Adolph Schmidt's home. Less than ten minutes later, he returned to the porch with two cups of tea. He handed one to the old man, and he drank it quickly. The American thanked the old man for his time, and shook his hand before heading down off the front porch. As he was walking toward his car parked on the side of the road, he turned back one final time to face the old man sitting alone on the porch.

"Herr Schmidt," he said. "You have been more helpful to me than you ever will know." And, then, he continued on and was gone.

Now, just a few minutes later, Adolph Schmidt sat alone on the porch thinking of all that had just happened. He tried to pull himself from the porch chair, but fell right back down again. He was dizzy and his eyesight was blurry. He reached for the now empty tea cup, but it fell and shattered on the porch floor.

He slumped further down in the chair, and felt his breath grow more and more shallow. His eyes were wide open as he took his final breath, and he stared forward.

In his mind, he stared into the glowing stone one last time.

Chapter Three

DALLAS, TX-PRESENT DAY

Rudolph Zeffner crouched in the closet, attempting to hide under some old coats and blankets. His heart was pounding so hard that he was sure that the man ransacking his home must surely be able to hear it. What's the point of living in the penthouse of a security building if something like this can happen in the middle of the day?

He was well into his eighth decade, although he looked much younger. He had a full head of hair, straight white teeth, and the skin of a man thirty years his junior which was the result of an almost fanatical dedication to daily moisturizing. Over the last twenty years he had grown to believe that this day would never actually come. He hoped that his heart would give out from panic before the man could find him.

A bird chirped loudly outside the study window. So loudly that Zeffner could hear it from his closet hiding spot. The sheer number and sounds of the bird life in Dallas never ceased to amaze him. He had actually taken up bird watching over the last few years—sitting for hours in stillness, and carefully documenting the different birds. The hobby of an old man, he thought.

He had only lived in Dallas a few years, but had been in the United States since 1962. By that point, most animosity that Americans felt toward the Germans over the War had been long forgotten. Instead he was an exotic man with an alluring accent. He came to the U.S. with a prestigious job at the Chicago Museum of Art as special assistant to the curator. He had always dreamed of living in the United States, and while nothing ever quite lives up to the expectations one builds for it, he had built himself a successful and happy life here.

While working at the museum in Chicago, he began teaching a few art history courses at DePaul and Loyola. It was there that he realized his true love of teaching. Or, maybe it wasn't the love of teaching as much as the way it felt to control a room, with the students hanging on his every word. He had loved the way they had looked at him—as if every word he spoke was pure brilliance. He found that the admiration he received from the students was almost intoxicating. Especially from the young male students.

In 1970 Rudolph Zeffner left Chicago and accepted a job at The Ohio State University as head of the religious art and history program. Over twenty years he built the religious art department at Ohio State into one of the top such programs in the world.

With the success of his program, Zeffner became one of the foremost experts on religious art in the world. He was frequently published, and even more frequently consulted for his opinion. During the "King Tut" craze of 1978 Zeffner appeared on all three network news magazine shows talking about the religious aspects of Egyptian art. If there was such a thing as a celebrity in the world of art history, Rudolph Zeffner was it.

With celebrity came all the trappings of success. The university paid him well, and the articles, books, and TV appearances supplemented his income nicely. As a frequent guest of the university president (he survived the reign of four of them), he met dignitaries and governors; corporate CEOs and Nobel Prize winners. And always, Zeffner would attend these events with a handsome young man as his guest.

The young men. Zeffner loved his work, and the art which he so dutifully studied, but of all the trappings of his life, the young men were his favorite. Zeffner learned early on that there was always a young graduate student who would enjoy his attention and company, and he went through them frequently—especially in the early years. But as he got older, the relationships lasted longer. He was with Gabe for over two years, and had now been with Kevin for nearly five.

Christ, he thought to himself. *I'm an old man who is finally ready to settle down, and it's now all about to end.*

And end in Texas of all places. Not that Zeffner particularly disliked the Lone Star State or its natives, but as an academic (and a liberal) he felt a need to show disdain for its "Red State" reputation and heritage. He had come here to build the collection of a privately funded museum of religious art.

Zeffner heard the door to his study being opened, and heavy footsteps on the hard wood floor outside the closet where he was hiding.

"Herr Zeffner," a heavy southern accent said. "I only want to have a talk with you. No reason to be scared."

The sound of the German title being said in such a deep southern accent was particularly jarring to Zeffner. What was it? Mississippi? Alabama? Something else?

Zeffner pulled a pen and note pad from his shirt pocket, and quickly wrote something on the piece of paper. He shoved the paper into the pocket of a tuxedo jacket hanging above him.

The closet door slowly opened. "I'm tired of this old man," the southern voice said.

Suddenly, the coats and blankets that made up his hiding place were ripped from him. "Ah," the southern man said with a smirk. "There's only so many places an old Nazi can hide."

Zeffner looked up at the man, realizing this was probably the last face he would ever see. He was wearing a short sleeved dress shirt, and dark pants that were about two sizes too large. Both arms were covered with crosses and other iconography of the Christian faith.

He dragged Zeffner from the closet. "Where is the light?" the man yelled.

"The light?" Zeffner asked. "Why, it's the middle of the day."

The southern man nearly shook with rage. "You know what I mean," he said through gritted teeth. "I want the gem of Holy Light."

"Sir, I have no idea of what you speak. I am an old man, and I cannot help you," Zeffner said, trying to hide the fear in his voice.

The southern man kicked him hard, and Zeffner screamed out in pain.

"I'll give you one more chance," he growled. "Where is the Holy Light?"

Zeffner looked up and smiled at the man. "Dummkopf," he said in a voice barely above a whisper. "You and your kind will never possess the Tzohar. Not that you people would understand it anyway. I'll die before it falls into the hands of a fundamentalist prick like you."

"That," the southern man said. "Can be easily arranged."

He pulled the gun from its holster, and pointed it at Zeffner's face.

"God, forgive me." Zeffner said closing his eyes.

"You're not going to God, you fucking Nazi," the southern man said as he fired two shots point blank into Rudolph Zeffner's head.

Chapter Four

COLUMBUS, OH-PRESENT DAY

Gabriel Patrick stared at the blinking cursor and white screen facing him. This was the third day in a row that he sat in front of his computer, seeking the words that never seemed to come.

He was attempting to write a book on the artistic endeavors of the Templar Knights. Not that he had any significant experience that qualified him to write such a book, or really any interest in the subject matter. But, rather, his agent Ellen said that the Templars were the "money" topic right now. Ellen made it perfectly clear that a "money" book was very important to his future as an author. So, Gabe sat and attempted to write—regardless of how futile it seemed.

He had written three previous books, all non-fiction and based on art history. A few of the more visionary professors (in his opinion, anyway) had made two of the books assigned reading in several art history courses. And, of course, Gabe had used the books in his own classes at Ohio State. (Well, the first two anyway—the third book was so bad, that not even Gabe could bring himself to assign it to a bunch of impressionable kids.)

So, Ellen had said this was pretty much his last chance. Not that a book on art history would ever top the *New York*

Times best seller list, but this one had to perform substantially better or she would have to drop him as a client. (Something about spending her time working with authors who could actually help her earn a living…) Not only that, but it was unlikely that even the academic publishers would be interested in him again.

Unfortunately, when Gabe couldn't write he instead tended to think. And recently he had been thinking a lot about his life. Specifically, how he was forty-two years old and nothing had quite turned out how he had planned.

In addition to the three books he had written over the last twelve years, Gabe had spent most of his adult life in academia. He was an assistant professor of art history at Ohio State for nearly fifteen years. Most people don't stay an *assistant* professor for fifteen years; in fact most are promoted by their seventh anniversary, and maybe co-chair of the department by their fifteenth. But, Gabe could never seem to master the acumen that was necessary to maneuver the political side of the university.

No matter how hard he tried, he just couldn't play the game. He understood the game; and he knew *how* to play the game. But, he just couldn't make himself do it. So, each time when he had the opportunity to suck up to some old pompous gas bag for a promotion, he instead would tell the guy just what he thought of him. So, he continued on as an assistant professor.

Finally, two years ago he had told one too many old pompous gas bags just what he thought of him. Unfortunately, this particular gas bag was also a vice provost. Gabe was notified that his contract would not be continued beyond the current academic quarter.

On his fortieth birthday he was unemployed, and the proud author of a tanking book. (Sales were so abysmal that Amazon wouldn't even provide a sales ranking.) It is tragic enough in the life of a gay man to turn forty, but to do so when feeling like such a loser was practically unbearable.

So, on the day after his fortieth birthday Gabe decided to do something he never had before—take a big chance. He took his entire life savings and a small inheritance from his grandfather, and bought a 112 year-old house in the Olde Towne East neighborhood of Columbus. His plan was to live on the upper two floors of the house, and use the ground floor as a combination antique shop and gallery. Finally, the only old gas bag he would have to suck up to was himself.

The business was a real struggle at first. For the first six months or so, he was positive he would have to declare bankruptcy any day. But just when he was ready to start searching for a cheap attorney to help begin the proceedings, Margo Hoffer walked in his door.

Margo Hoffer came into his shop looking for a set of

glassware. Specifically, she was looking for a cobalt blue design made by the now defunct Hazel Atlas glass company. Margo was in her seventies, and had very fond memories of the "good glasses" that her mother used only on special occasions. Margo thought the glasses were the most beautiful things she had ever seen.

Margo's mother had always promised that the glasses would belong to her one day, but in the early 1960s the family home burned down, and all their personal possessions were lost. Even with the lost photos, clothing, and childhood toys, Margo was crushed by the loss of the glasses. She told Gabe that she had spent most of the past forty years searching antique store after antique store trying to find the beloved glasses.

She showed Gabe a photo from a Christmas dinner in 1956 where the glasses could be clearly seen on the table. Gabe told her he had some contacts that specialized in glassware, and he would see what he could do. Gabe kept a copy of the photo, and told Margo he would call her in a few days to let her know if he had any luck.

Gabe had attended a symposium in Detroit a few years back on Depression-era glass, and remembered a collector from Seattle who specialized in Cobalt Blue pieces. Personally, Gabe found the style pretty tacky, but it seemed to have a popular following. With all his faults, disorganization was not one of them, and Gabe always took impeccable notes at every lecture he attended.

He found the man's contact information in his notes, and gave him a call. Gabe described the glasses, and faxed the collector a copy of the photo. Within a few hours the man had e-mailed him information about another collector who had several sets of the glasses. Within a few hours of that, he had reached a deal with the second collector to buy eight of the glasses for $700, nearly every dime he had. He drove to Wheeling that afternoon to pick up the purchase.

Gabe figured he would sell the glasses to Margo for $1000, which would be a healthy profit, and would keep the wolves from the door for at least a few more days. He called Margo the next day, and she said she would be at his shop early the next morning.

She was not joking about early, as she was ringing his bell at 7:00 a.m. the next morning. Gabe brought her inside and handed her a tissue paper wrapped glass. Margo unwrapped it and immediately burst into tears. Gabe was startled.

"Aren't these the glasses?" he asked hesitantly.

"Oh, yes. Oh, yes," she sobbed. "I just never thought I'd see them again."

She pulled herself together, and opened up her purse and handed Gabe a check for $5000.

"Wow," he said, amazed by the amount of the check.

"This is way too much money. I can't accept this much."

"Of course you can," Margo said, cracking a smile. "Young man, I have plenty of money, but you have given me something worth much more than cash. You've given me back a piece of my life I thought was gone forever."

A few minutes later, Gabe helped her load the glasses into her car and watched her drive off. A few days later he received a call from a man who had been referred to him by Mrs. Hoffer. He was looking for a type of pocket watch. Gabe was also able to locate his item as well.

A few days after that, he was contacted by another referral from either Mrs. Hoffer or the pocket watch man. And then another; and another. (It reminded him of the old shampoo commercial from the 80s…) Within a few months, Gabe had made over $25,000 in pure profit.

For the first time in his working life, he felt legitimately successful. Not just because he was making good money for a change, but because he felt like he was genuinely helping people. He loved seeing the look on a person's face when he handed them something that they thought had been lost forever.

Gabe's thoughts were interrupted by the sound of incoming e-mail. It was a forwarded news story from a former colleague. He stared in disbelief at the headline in front of him.

"World Renowned Art Historian Murdered in Robbery"

Chapter Five

G abe sat at the screen, transfixed by the news story in front of him.

Dallas, TX-Rudolph Zeffner, a world-renowned art historian and expert on religious art and artifacts was murdered Thursday morning in what was believed to be a home invasion and robbery. Zeffner was found shot to death in his twentieth floor condominium in the Turtle Creek neighborhood of Dallas.

Zeffner, who immigrated from Germany in 1962, was one of the world's foremost experts on religious art and iconography, and was frequently consulted by the media on the subject. He had appeared on the Today Show, Good Morning America, and The Tonight Show with Johnny Carson. He moved to Dallas in 2004 and was currently working with a private trust to develop a museum of religious art near downtown Dallas.

Rudy was dead. Gabe could barely believe what he was reading. Granted, the man was in his eighties so his death really should not be so shocking, but Gabe still had a hard time fathoming it. He was especially shocked regarding the way he died—shot and killed during a robbery in his condo. It was unbelievable. Gabe always figured that Rudy would die of a heart attack at a circuit party in Miami, or Palm

Springs or somewhere equally flamboyant. You know—die as he had lived.

Gabe did a quick Google search to see what additional information he could find. A few other news sites carried the same basic story. He found Rudy's obituary in the *Dallas Morning News*. It said he was being cremated the next day, and requested that in lieu of flowers a donation be made to the Survivor Mitzvah Project, which provides financial aid to Jewish survivors of the Holocaust. It said that he is survived by his partner, Kevin Hurst.

Gabe read that last line several times. *He is survived by his partner, Kevin Hurst.*

There was a time when Gabe could not imagine his life without Rudy, but over the last several years they spoke less and less frequently. He met Rudolph Zeffner in 1984 when he was a graduate student at Ohio State. Gabe was in the religious art and history program, and Zeffner was the head of the department. Even though he was in his sixties at the time, Gabe found him incredibly charming and handsome. He was amazed by his genius, and captivated by his charms.

Gabe tried not to be flattered by the extra attention that "Rudy" (as he insisted his young proteges call him) lavished on him. After all, it was well known that each year he chose a young, male "pet" for whom he lavished his praise, attention...yet, Gabe couldn't help but to still feel special because of it.

Gabe was Rudy's "companion" (the term Zeffner preferred) for nearly two years—the entire academic year and
then some. It was a fun relationship, and Gabe got to meet
a lot of important people at the university and within the art
world. He loved the way people looked at Rudy when he was
speaking, and he felt a little of the warmth of the spotlight
that was always on Rudy.

But, like most relationships with an older experienced
man and a younger star struck paramour forty years his
junior, it just was not meant to last. Gabe was quickly
replaced by a younger and more fawning version of himself. But, it was really OK—Gabe felt richer and better for
the experience, and had no regrets. It had been a good run,
and it was not as though Gabe thought it would last forever.
Plus, he felt a little special—most of Rudy's student affairs
lasted only a semester or so.

Zeffner left his post at Ohio State in 1991, and moved
on to several expensive consulting gigs with some of the
world's most prestigious museums. He authored dozens of
books, and was called on by the media whenever there was
some art-focused story in the news. He was a true star of
the art world.

Gabe and Rudy stayed in contact after their relationship
ended, and spoke often. They had in-depth conversations

about whatever hot topics happened to be going on in the art world, and of course, gossiped about mutual acquaintances. He knew that Rudy genuinely liked and respected him. He was somewhat surprised sometimes about how much that meant to him.

Rudy also served as Gabe's professional mentor with limited success. He was always giving Gabe advice about things he should do to increase his visibility at the university and get closer to a promotion.

"You've got to play the game," Rudy would say. "It's the way the world works."

"I know, I know," a frustrated Gabe would say. "But, I just hate sucking up to those bastards. I just don't see how you do it."

"Liebchen," Rudy would sigh. "You're talking to a man who worked for the Nazis. A pompous university bureaucrat is nothing in comparison."

After finishing his Doctorate, Gabe spent a year or so working for the Cincinnati Museum of Art, but then landed back at Ohio State teaching in Rudy's old department. By then, Zeffner had moved on to bigger and better things, and his successor at Ohio State did not hold Gabe in the same esteem as his former *companion* had. But, it was a steady job, and with an advanced degree in art history it was about the best someone in his position could expect.

Zeffner had made quite the impression—both personally and professionally—on Gabe. He had picked up a few of his mentor's eccentricities—a short tempered approach to clerical personnel, but also a penchant for an annual romantic fling with one of his graduate assistants. He told himself that it was all part of their learning experience—just like it had been for him.

That's how he had met Kevin—nearly twenty years after his relationship with Rudy ended, and after more fleeting *companions* than he could even now remember. Kevin Hurst was an MFA candidate pursuing an advanced degree in classical piano. His dream was to become a concert pianist; traveling with a world renowned symphony. As part of his MFA program, he was required to do a stint in the art history program.

It was during that time that Kevin became one of Gabe's graduate assistants, and while not the brightest or most talented grad students he had ever had, he more than compensated for it in other ways. He was funny, gregarious, and very good looking. (In fact, much more good looking than Gabe ever thought he deserved in a *companion* of his own.) And, as a former NCAA soccer player, he kept the lithe, tight body of an athlete.

Along about their second year together, Gabe started to think of their relationship as more than just a fling, and really believed that they could be together for the long haul. Shortly after their third anniversary they ran into Zeffner at a party in New York. Rudy had been his normal, charming self and Gabe had thought little of it. But, as he later found out, Rudy and Kevin continued talking. Gabe was completely surprised the day, months later, when Kevin came to him and told him he was leaving—to be with Rudy.

Gabe was crushed. Not only was he losing what he thought was the love of his life, but he was also losing the man who had the greatest impact on his adult life and career. Shortly after Kevin left, Rudy called him.

"Don't dwell on this as if it were your fault, or if there was something you could have done differently, liebchen," Rudy said. "Young men are always attracted to fame and power—it's not their fault. It's like blaming a pig for wallowing in the mud. It hurts now, but that will fade, and someday you'll forgive us both. As I've always told you, if you ever really loved someone, a part of you will always love them. Regardless of whatever pain they may temporarily cause you."

"That's bullshit, and you know it," Gabe replied quietly, consciously concentrating on not raising his voice. He did not want to give Rudy the satisfaction. "Yeah, Kevin's young and shallow. I get that. What's your excuse?"

"What can I say?" Rudy asked. "I enjoy the mud as well."

Then Zeffner hung up the phone. That was five years

ago, and they had only talked a few times since then. They ran into each other at professional conferences once in a while, and Rudy never failed to send him a birthday card. But, other than that, on a single day, what had been the two most important relationships of Gabe's life simply stopped.

He always believed that at some point he and Rudy might actually be able to regain a friendship again, and he had even stopped himself from calling several times. On the other hand, he had no intention of ever speaking to Kevin again. Gabe always assumed at some point Rudy would grow tired of Kevin and discard him like all the others—like he had Gabe. But, as the years passed, he began to wonder if that was just his own bitter wishful thinking.

But, now it was all academic. Rudy was dead, and there was no chance of ever making amends. He felt a tear roll down his cheek, and he realized for the first time in many years just how important the old Kraut had been to him.

Bang! Bang! He jumped suddenly as he heard the pounding of the antique door knocker against his front door. The knock was quick; almost frantic. Gabe got up from his desk and walked to the door. He pulled the curtain aside to see who it was.

"Jesus," he said in an amazed tone.

It was Kevin.

Chapter Six

When the front door of the old brick house opened, Kevin practically pushed Gabe out of the way to get inside.

"Kevin, what the hell?" Gabe started to say.

"I think I might have been followed here," Kevin said, breathing hard and peeking around the curtains on the door window.

"Followed? What are you talking about? " Gabe asked in an exasperated tone. "Why aren't you in Dallas?"

"Rudy's dead," Kevin said quietly.

"I know," Gabe said, almost as quietly. "Mark Stuhl emailed me, and I read the news story online. I'm so sorry." He genuinely meant it.

"He was murdered," Kevin said in a hoarse whisper.

"I know," Gabe said. "It was a robbery, I read about it in the Dallas paper."

"No, it wasn't a robbery," Kevin said coldly. "Everyone is saying that it was, but it was something else. Someone killed Rudy for some other reason."

"Kevin, that doesn't make any sense at all," Gabe said, putting his hand on Kevin's shoulder. "Why would anyone want to kill Rudy?" Of course, as soon as he said the words out loud, he thought of a few times in his not so distant past where he may have entertained the option himself. He quickly shook the thought from his head. "Someone probably thought there was valuable art or antiques in the house and broke in to steal them. The article said that police believe Rudy probably surprised them."

"No!" Kevin said, clearly agitated. "There was nothing stolen, anything of value is still in the condo. Whoever broke in intended to kill Rudy."

Gabe looked at Kevin with a concern that he never believed he could feel for him again. Maybe there was actually something to Rudy's platitudes about always loving someone you once had. He pulled him in tighter to him. At first, Kevin resisted the effort, but then gave in to the embrace.

"Come on," Gabe said. "I think we both could use a drink."

Chapter Seven

They sat at a table in the small Short North wine bar and said nothing for several minutes, during which time Kevin downed two glasses of wine. They had come to this place often while they were together.

"This place really hasn't changed much at all, has it?" Kevin said, more as a statement than a question.

"Ok," Gabe said. "Now that things are a little calmer, why don't you explain that episode back at my house."

Kevin said nothing, but reached into the messenger bag he had carried with him since arriving at Gabe's and pulled out a folded piece of paper. He tossed the paper across the table to Gabe.

Gabe unfolded the sheet to read it.

Not as it seems, or as you will be told. Look to Gabriel for the light of understanding. AH-JAD, A-CHI, TSAH, YEH-HES, A-CHIN, JEHA

Gabe looked up from the note, and stared at Kevin with an obviously confused expression.

"I found this in the pocket of his favorite tuxedo jacket," Kevin said, much more calmly as the wine took effect. "He wanted to be wearing that old tux when he was cremated. I was getting it ready to take to the mortuary, when I found it in the pocket."

"What does it mean?" Gabe asked.

"I was hoping you could tell me," Kevin said. "I assumed you were the 'Gabriel' in question that would provide the so-called *light of understanding*."

Kevin said the words with an accusing tone that he did not quite mean, yet still could not help himself from using. He had always been jealous of Rudy's intellectual bond with Gabe. Finding this note when faced with the shock of Rudy's death, only intensified that feeling.

"Kevin," Gabe said. "I haven't spoken to Rudy for months. I have no idea what this could mean, but maybe I'm not the *Gabriel* he's talking about."

"Who else could it be?" Kevin asked, skeptically.

"Well, being an expert on religious art and icons, Rudy was always fascinated by the stories of the Angel Gabriel," Gabe said, sounding much more professorial than he intended. "Not only was Gabriel one of the only angels actually named in the Bible, but he also played a huge role in the three major Western religions—Judaism, Christianity, and Islam."

"So what Gabe," Kevin said somewhat angrily. "You think Rudy wants me to talk to an angel to find out who killed him? What the hell kind of advice is that?"

"No," Gabe said calmly. "That's not what I'm saying. You know how much Rudy loved all this cryptic crap. He always did consider himself some sort of treasure-hunting adventure character. Maybe it's just Rudy being Rudy."

Kevin sat quietly and considered what Gabe was saying.

"Plus," Gabe said. "Do you even know how old this note is? Rudy bought that tux back in the seventies when he was invited to a party at Studio 54. It might not even have anything to do with death."

"God," Kevin said. "You sound like the damn Dallas Police. I called them right after I found the note, and they just blew me off."

"Of course, everyone thinks I am just the hysterical faggot who lost his sugar daddy."

Gabe looked intently at Kevin, and felt genuine empathy for the man. After all, this was a person he really had once loved very much, and it still hurt him to see Kevin in this much pain.

"Ok," Gabe said rising, and throwing two twenties on the table to cover their bill. "It's obvious you're serious about this. Let's go back to my house and figure this thing out."

Chapter Eight

A s they pulled up in front of his house, Gabe had a feeling something was wrong. He quickly parked the car on the street and bounded out and up his front steps. His front door was slightly ajar; it had been kicked open.

"Jesus," Gabe said. "What the hell happened?"

Kevin was standing close behind him, as he slowly pushed the door open.

"Be careful. They might still be in there."

Gabe had not considered the *they* before then, but Kevin's comment suddenly brought the reality home to him. Someone (*they*) had broken into his house; in the middle of the day, when he had hardly been gone an hour.

Gabe and Kevin walked slowly into the foyer, but leaving the front door wide open behind them.

"The police are on their way," Gabe yelled to no one in particular, his voice cracking at the end. "I've called the police!"

Just then, Gabe and Kevin heard the back screen door slam shut. They looked at each other with wide, startled eyes. Before stopping to think, they both ran toward the back door in the kitchen.

They got to the kitchen door, just to see the driver's door slamming shut on a dark colored sedan. The car peeled out down the alley that bordered the back of Gabe's property. Gabe tried to see the license plate, but the car was moving too quickly for him to make out any of the numbers, or even its state of issue.

"Damn," he said in a hoarse whisper.

Gabe and Kevin walked back into the house. The place had been ransacked. Drawers had been emptied and their contents dumped to the floor. He did a quick visual inventory; all of the antiques and art in the gallery appeared to be there, and $46 in cash was still in the caddy on his desk. Then Gabe noticed something was missing.

"They got my laptop," he said, looking around for any other missing items.

"They followed me," Kevin said, his tone rising. "They followed me to Columbus. They want to kill me like they killed Rudy."

"Kevin," Gabe said sharply. "We don't know any such thing. This is not a great neighborhood. It's my own damn fault for not setting the alarm before we left."

"You really can't be serious," Kevin said, his tone every bit as sharp. "Rudy was murdered. I came to you with a note where Rudy told us that things weren't as they appeared, and within two hours of me getting here your house was ransacked—just like when Rudy was killed."

Gabe had no response. Every rational thought he had

rejected this entire thing. However, even he was beginning to realize that things were getting really weird.

"Gabe," Kevin said. "How many robbers would break into a house and only take a computer? Especially when there's cash sitting right there next to it?"

"I don't know, Kevin. I just don't know," Gabe said, slowly shaking his head.

"Whatever they were looking for when they killed Rudy, they're still looking for. And, they obviously think I—and now you—must know something about it."

"Ok," Gabe said. "Let's say that's true. What in the world could be so important that someone would kill Rudy and follow you from Texas to Ohio to get?"

"I have absolutely no idea," Kevin said. "But, I have a feeling that Rudy knew exactly what they were looking for. And, I think by leaving that note he wanted me—well, *us*—to know as well."

Gabe was suddenly hit with the ridiculousness of the situation, and laughed out loud. "Yes," he said, still laughing. "That would be just like the old German bastard, huh?"

Kevin was at first angered by Gabe's reaction, but soon found the laughter contagious. The whole situation was just so ludicrous, laughter seemed the only reasonable emotion.

"Ok," Gabe said, pulling himself together. "If we're going to do this, we're going to need some help."

"From who?" Kevin asked.

"Well, we're going to start with the police," Gabe said.

Chapter Nine

The woman quickly ran up the steps of Gabe's front porch.

"So, what happened," she asked. "You piss off some trick or something?"

"You know, Molly," Gabe said. "I'm not exactly in a joking mood this afternoon."

Molly Newman was an officer in the Columbus Police Department. Gabe had met her shortly after moving into the neighborhood. He had joined the Olde Towne East community association, and she was the police liaison to the group. She and her partner Vickie lived a few blocks from Gabe.

"Oh, come on, Gabe," Molly said, walking up the front porch steps. "It's times like this when you need to keep your sense of humor. You always need to keep a sense of humor."

Her blue eyes sparkled, and she gave him a mischievous grin. Molly was not exactly a lipstick lesbian, nor was she butch. Gabe always thought she looked like a woman that could easily be driving a mini van through a Kroger parking lot in the suburbs. He doubted that most people she came into contact with on a daily basis would ever think she was a lesbian.

"So, who's your friend?" She asked, motioning toward Kevin.

"This is Kevin Hurst," Gabe hesitated for a moment. "He's an old friend who is visiting from out of town."

Gabe thought he saw a look of understanding in Molly's expression. They had gone out for drinks occasionally after the association meetings, and he was sure that he must have mentioned the whole Gabe/Kevin/Rudy triangle at least a few times. (No matter how hard he tried, a few—or several—beers always seemed to result in a retelling of his own personal soap opera.)

"It's nice to meet you, Kevin," Molly said, extending her hand and smiling at him. In her line of work, she understood the importance of discretion.

"What time did you discover the break-in?" Molly asked, pulling out her notebook. In a split second she shifted from joking friend to serious professional.

"We got back around 3:00," Gabe said. "We had only been gone about an hour, so it happened pretty quickly."

"Have you done an inventory to determine if anything is missing?"

"The only thing that seems to be missing is my laptop computer. All of my gallery items and antique pieces are still there."

"That's not too surprising," Molly said, still jotting down notes in her book. "You can't exactly expect some east side crack head to know the value of art. The laptop is a lot easier to pawn."

"Yes," Gabe said. "but, they left cash laying on the desk right next to where the laptop had been. I can't imagine someone robbing a house to get drug money passing up easy cash."

"Yes, that does sound really odd." Molly stopped writing, and looked at Gabe.

"Molly, Kevin thinks…" Gabe started to say, then stopped himself and restarted. "Kevin *and I* think there may be something more to this."

Gabe invited Molly into the house, and the three of them sat in the living room. Gabe and Kevin took turns telling the story of Rudy's death, the associated break in, the odd note, Kevin's panicked trip to Columbus, and finally the robbery at Gabe's.

Molly finished reading the note, and handed it back to Gabe.

"You two do understand how crazy this whole story sounds, don't you?"

"Yes, of course we do," Gabe said. "But you have to admit the whole thing seems really weird."

"I'm not sure how weird it actually is. Two houses being broken into and ransacked in two different urban neighborhoods, in two different cities? I'm willing to bet I can find similar break-ins in Chicago, Detroit, and Atlanta on the very same day. Think those might be related too?"

As soon as she said it, Molly regretted the sarcastic tone.

Gabe refolded the note and put it into his pocket. Of course he understood how ridiculous their story sounded. He had been saying the same thing himself all afternoon, but as he told the story out loud to Molly, the more he began thinking there might really be something to all this.

"What about the note?" Kevin asked, defensive and angry. "What about the dark car we saw speeding away? That didn't look like a crack head's car to me."

"Ok, guys," Molly said, in her most diplomatic tone. "I'll admit that there are some odd coincidental elements here. But, I also know you both lost someone very close to you to the worst kind of violence. Do me a favor and at least consider that may be playing a part in your interpretation of all this."

Gabe and Kevin looked at each other, then at Molly, but said nothing.

Molly rose from the couch and began walking toward the front door. "I'll get the police report filed, and we'll keep a look out for your laptop at the neighborhood pawn shops."

"Thanks," Gabe said. "I appreciate your help with this."

"Also," Molly said, almost as an after thought. "My sergeant is from Dallas. He spent fifteen years on the force there. Maybe I can get him to call down and find out what's going on in the investigation of your friend's murder. Maybe we can see if there are any similarities between that break-in and this one."

"Thanks," Gabe said. "That would really mean a lot to us."

"Yes," Kevin said, sounding relieved. "Thank you."

Molly stepped out onto the porch, then turned back to look at Gabe and Kevin.

"Well, I'll say one thing," she said, the mischievous sparkle returning to her eyes. "You boys certainly do love the drama."

Chapter Ten

Kevin watched as Molly drove off in the police cruiser. "So, what exactly are we supposed to do now?"

"Research," Gabe said calmly. "I've been thinking about the note, and I have some ideas about those strange words. But first we need to locate a computer and an Internet connection."

* * * *

Twenty minutes later Gabe and Kevin were sitting in front of a terminal in the computer center at one of the less frequently used branches of the Columbus Public Library.

"The more I thought about the code in the note, the more it seemed somehow familiar," Gabe said. "I think it may be Navajo."

"Navajo? You mean like the Indian tribe?"

"Well, technically, I believe it's considered a nation instead of a tribe, but yes—that's exactly what I mean."

"What in the world makes you think it's Navajo writing?" Kevin asked, somewhat skeptically.

"Well, for one thing, I've seen it written before," Gabe said. "And, for another, I know that it was a fascination of Rudy's."

"What? I've never heard him mention Navajo Indians before, and trust me—I've heard him ramble on about a lot of things."

"Rudy was very interested in the Navajo, or more specifically, Navajo Code Talkers," Gabe explained. "The Navajo language was used as a secret code by the Allies in World War Two. It was the only code that the Germans were never able to crack."

"And Rudy was interested in this?" Kevin asked.

"Yeah, I think he always felt somewhat humbled by it. I think he also enjoyed the idea of the German High Command being played for fools."

What Gabe did not explain to Kevin was that Rudy used to leave little notes for him written in Navajo code. Somewhat as a joke, but still somewhat romantic. It was like a secret they shared. Gabe realized that he must not have done the same thing with Kevin. Maybe there was no standard play book after all. He shook the thought from his mind; now was not the time to dwell on this.

Gabe entered a few text strings in the search engine, and several seconds later he was looking at an online declassified Code Talker dictionary.

He looked at the code written in Rudy's hand: *AH-JAD, A-CHI, TSAH, YEH-HES, A-CHIN, JEHA.*

Gabe looked at the first set of characters, and scanned

the dictionary. Each phrase separated by a comma seemed to correspond to a letter. *AH-JAD* translated to the English letter "L." *A-CHI* translated to the letter "I."

L-I-N-I-N-G

"Lining?" Gabe asked underneath his breath. "Lining?"

"Lining? What are you talking about?" Kevin asked impatiently.

"Kevin, where did you say you found the note from Rudy?"

"In the pocket of his tuxedo. I already told you that. I was getting it ready to take to the mortuary."

"I think the code in the note is telling us to check out the lining of Rudy's jacket," Gabe said, shaking his head. "When is he scheduled to be cremated?"

"Tomorrow. He's scheduled to be cremated tomorrow, and the memorial service is scheduled for the day after."

Gabe stood up suddenly, quickly scooping up his note papers into his messenger bag. "We've got to go right now," he said.

"Go where exactly?" Kevin asked.

"We need to get to Dallas right away. We need to check out the lining of that tuxedo jacket before Rudy is cremated."

Chapter Eleven

A fter leaving the library, Gabe and Kevin headed back to Gabe's house to pack an overnight bag for the unexpected trip to Dallas. They arrived at Port Columbus airport less than an hour later. American Airlines had a non-stop flight from Columbus to Dallas leaving at 8:40. Only first class seats were available—at nearly $2000 each.

After getting settled on the plane, Gabe closed his eyes and tried to process everything that was happening to him. It seemed almost impossible to believe that it had been only a little more than six hours ago that Kevin had shown up at his door. So many things—so many weird things—had happened since then.

"What could he be leading us to?" Kevin asked suddenly, seemingly as much to himself as to Gabe.

"I honestly don't have a clue. You're the one that's been with him for the last five years. You should have a better idea than I do."

"What's that supposed to mean?"

"It means what it means, Kevin. I'm not sure what you want from me."

Gabe leaned his head against the seat rest and closed his eyes. He was angry with himself for his reaction, but he could not help himself. Since all this happened he had been too preoccupied to remember just how angry he had been with Kevin and Rudy. But it all seemed to come flooding back to him in that moment.

His eyes were closed, but he could feel Kevin looking at him from the neighboring seat.

"Gabe," Kevin said hesitantly. "Rudy really did feel awful about what happened with us. I do too."

Gabe opened his eyes and looked at him; not sure how to respond.

"Do you want me to tell you that it's all OK now? Because I'm not sure I can do that," Gabe said.

"I know," Kevin said quietly. "I just felt I should say it."

Kevin sat back against the seat and closed his eyes as well.

Gabe looked at him, and as much as he wanted to be furious with Kevin, he just did not have it in him tonight.

"Kevin, I am glad you said it," Gabe said. "And, it surprises the hell out of me—but, for some strange reason, it does help."

Chapter Twelve

The plane landed in Dallas shortly after eleven, and it was nearly Midnight before they pulled out of DFW's rental car facility.

They decided to spend the night at a hotel; Kevin said he did not feel comfortable going back to the condo in Turtle Creek so soon. Gabe did not say anything to Kevin, but he imagined the condo would still be a crime scene anyway. So, it was probably best to avoid that whole scene.

They spent the night in separate rooms at the Melrose Hotel in the Oak Lawn district near downtown. They both woke up early to a bright, sunny Texas Autumn morning. By 8:00 A.M. they were sitting at the Crossroads Market on Cedar Springs drinking coffee.

"Well, are you ready to do this?"

"No," Kevin replied. "But to be perfectly honest, I'm not exactly sure what we're going to do anyway."

"Yeah," Gabe sighed. "Me either."

They drove to the Lansing Funeral Chapel in the Knox-Henderson area. Lansing had gained some prominence within the Dallas gay community years ago when they were one of the few funeral homes that would openly handle AIDS deaths early in the epidemic. Most funeral homes at the time were frightened of working with AIDS victims, because so little was known about how the disease was actually spread. It was the dark ages of the disease, but it did not deter the Lansings from doing what they thought was right. After losing so many friends over the years, it did not surprise Gabe that this is where Rudy would have decided to make his final arrangements.

They opened the front door of the mortuary, and were announced by a ringing bell. Within a few seconds a man who looked to be in his sixties approached from another room.

"Good morning, may I help you?" the man asked Gabe and Kevin.

"Yes," Kevin said, his voice cracking slightly. "I'm Kevin Hurst, and this is my friend Gabriel Patrick. I am—*I was*—Rudolph Zeffner's partner."

"Oh, yes Mr. Hurst," the man said warmly and extending his hand. "I'm Peter Lansing. I am so sorry for your loss, and we're here to help anyway we can in this difficult time."

"I'd like to see Rudy," Kevin said. "One last time."

The older man gave Kevin a sympathetic smile. "Well, we hadn't planned for a scheduled viewing, but I'm sure we can arrange something for this evening if that's convenient."

"No," Kevin said, somewhat firmer than he had intended. "I really want to see Rudy now."

Peter Lansing was noticeably surprised by Kevin's

request.

"Of course, sir," he said in a comforting tone. "We have him dressed in the clothing requested for cremation, but haven't prepared him for a public viewing. I just don't want you to be troubled."

"Trust me," Kevin said. "Rudy not wearing makeup is the least of my troubles now."

Lansing seemed to understand the determination in Kevin's request. "Give me a few moments sir, and I'll have Mr. Zeffner brought to one of our viewing rooms."

Lansing made a quick call, and within ten minutes he was leading Kevin and Gabe into a closed room off the main hallway. The room was small, with a plain wooden casket on a pedestal at one end. The carpet was a deep gold color, and the walls were covered in an antique looking wallpaper. Floral sofas lined the walls of the room, and heavy velvet curtains hung from each window.

"Sort of Country French, for the funeral set, huh?" Gabe said under his breath.

Kevin smiled slightly, grateful for Gabe's attempt to lighten the mood.

As they walked closer to the casket, Kevin and Gabe got their first look at Rudy.

"Oh, my God," Kevin said, his voice breaking. "I can't really believe that he's dead."

"I know, Kevin," Gabe said softly. "But we have to do this; we have to follow where Rudy is leading us. He wants us to do this."

Kevin shook his head in agreement, and breathed in deeply. They stood in front of Rudy's open casket. His face was ashen, and heavy dark circles surrounded his eyes. Always proud of his relatively youthful appearance, Rudolph Zeffner looked every bit of his eight-plus decades right now.

Kevin reached down and touched Rudy's hand. It felt cold, lifeless, and no longer seemed to have any connection to the man he loved.

"Ok," Gabe said, nervously sucking in breath through his teeth. "I guess it's time to do this."

He gently stuck his hand inside the front of Rudy's jacket, and carefully moved it over the lining; searching for anything that felt unusual. Finding nothing on the right side of the jacket, he moved to the left. He was about to give up, when he felt something small and hard under the lining near the inside pocket.

He gently pulled at the seams of the lining, and pushed the small object through the hole he had torn.

"What is it?" Kevin asked.

Gabe looked at him with an expression that bordered on surprise and disbelief.

"It's a key," he said.

Chapter Thirteen

Within the hour, Gabe and Kevin were back at the Crossroads Market drinking more coffee. Neither one had said barely a word in the car on the way back, and that silence continued through their third cup of coffee of the day.

Gabe pulled the key they found in the lining of Rudy's tux jacket, and turned it over in his hands. He stared at it intently, as if looking at it hard enough would provide some sort of meaning. He read and reread the characters "FNBT" and "826" engraved on the face of the key.

"So," Kevin asked. "What do you think it means?"

"I'm not exactly sure," Gabe said, pulling out his cell phone. "But, I'm willing to bet the engraving on this key can tell us something."

He started up the web browser on the phone, and launched its search engine. He enters "FNBT" as the search criteria, and within a few seconds thousands of hits were returned. While there were a variety of suggestions, the most frequently returned result for FNBT was the First National Bank of Texas.

"The First National Bank of Texas," Gabe said, reading the results to Kevin. "I think this may be the key to a safe deposit box. Did Rudy have an account there?"

"Not that I'm aware of, but Rudy and I always kept our finances separate."

Gabe enters another string of characters into the phone's search engine, then waits for the results.

"Damn. This will take forever."

"What's wrong?"

"According to their web site, there are 57 FNBT branches within the DFW Metroplex, it would take forever to track down which branch," Gabe said, handing his phone to Kevin.

"It's this one," Kevin said, pointing to a photo on the web site's home page. "The main branch downtown. I didn't realize what it was, but Rudy was always going on and on about that building whenever we were downtown. Something about the 'Greek revival architecture'. It would make sense that would be the bank he chose."

Gabe looked at Kevin and smiled. Kevin returned the smile.

"Ok," Gabe said, breaking the moment. "Finish up your coffee—we're going to the bank."

Chapter Fourteen

Gabe and Kevin parked the rental car in a surface lot a few blocks from the downtown main branch of the First National Bank of Texas. The bank was located on Commerce Street, just a few blocks from Dealey Plaza.

Gabe had been to Dallas several times, but had never visited the spot where John F. Kennedy was assassinated. He always intended to go when he was visiting, but could just never seem to fit it into his schedule. Gabe was sure that Rudy had made time to visit the Sixth Floor Museum—and probably, multiple times. Rudy was fascinated by learning about history, and the more tragic that history, the more it seemed to interest him.

Gabe and Kevin walked into the main lobby of the bank, and headed straight to the information desk.

"Good morning," Gabe said, smiling to the woman at the desk. "I need to get access to a safe deposit box—number 826."

"Of course, sir," the woman said, returning Gabe's smile. "Your name?"

"Gabriel Patrick and Kevin Hurst," Gabe said confidently. He was sure to give both their names, because he still was not sure Rudy had even intended for him to be here. He sounded much more confident than he felt.

"Thank you sir," the woman said. "May I see your iden-tification?"

Both Gabe and Kevin showed her their driver's license, and she studied each license, then looked at each of them.

"Just a moment please, gentleman," she said, rising from behind the information desk.

She walked back to the area behind the bank tellers, and began typing some information into a computer terminal. Gabe and Kevin watched her as she looked at the screen, then looked up at both of them across the room. She motioned for another woman nearby to come over to her. Both women looked at the terminal screen.

"Am I the only one starting to get a little nervous?" Kevin asked.

"I was nervous when we walked in here," Gabe said.

The woman walked away from the computer terminal, and began heading back to the main lobby where Gabe and Kevin were waiting.

"Thank you, Mr. Patrick and Mr. Hurst," she said approaching them. "Everything seems to be in order, and both your names are on the access list for the box. So, would you like to follow me to the vault?"

Gabe and Kevin both did their best to not look relieved, and followed the woman into an elevator off the lobby. The elevator went down one floor, and opened into a hallway in front of the safe.

The woman tapped in several numbers on a keyboard at the metal door, then placed her index finger on a biometric sensor next to the number pad. The metal door released, and Gabe and Kevin followed her into the ante room of the safe.

"I'll just need you to insert your key at the same time as mine," she said, putting her master key into one of the slots on the outside of box number 826.

Gabe inserted the key he held into the other slot, and both he and the woman turned their key at the same time. The door to the safety deposit box opened, revealing a smaller grey metal lock box on the inside. The woman pulled the lock box out of its shelf, and handed it to Gabe.

"Would you like to use one of our private reviewing rooms?" the woman asked.

"Yes," both Gabe and Kevin answered simultaneously, and somewhat louder than either intended. The woman gave them a slightly surprised look.

The woman led them into one of the small reviewing rooms off the main hallway, and motioned to a small table with four chairs.

"Make yourself comfortable, and take as long as you need," she said, walking out of the room and closing the door behind her.

"Ok," Gabe said. "Let's see what Rudy felt was so important that he had to put us through this little exercise."

Gabe opened the grey metal box, and pulled out its only contents—a white business-sized envelope. Gabe opened the sealed envelope and pulled out two handwritten pages, what looked to be a business card, and a large amount of cash.

"Jesus," Kevin said. "There's got to be thousands of dollars here!"

Gabe picked up the pages and unfolded them. He stared intently at the first page.

"What is it?"

"It's a letter," Gabe said quietly. "Addressed to the both of us."

Chapter Fifteen

G abe and Kevin sat beside each other with the letter centered on the table between them. They both read silently:

Dearest Kevin and Gabriel,

My liebchens, if you are reading this letter, I am now most likely dead. Or, I have finally decided that my whole story is nothing more than the delusions of an old man. But either way, I'm glad to finally tell you my tale.

I'm counting on the fact that you two are together. I'm not sure how I will do it yet, but somehow I will leave a message to you Kevin, to seek out Gabe. I hope that your differences can be put aside long enough to come together to do as I ask.

I've rewritten this letter nearly twenty times since the first draft in 1986. After I met you Gabriel, I knew that I finally had met someone who could share my secret. Kevin, I later realized that you must also be part of this quest. Regardless of what has happened between the three of us, the two of you are the closest I've come to having family in many years, and the only ones I can trust with this task.

Over sixty years ago, the most glorious treasure in the history of the world came into my possession. I know I'm prone to hyperbole (as Kevin so lovingly calls me an "old drama queen"), but I'm not exaggerating when I tell you this—it will change the entire world. On a Winter's night in 1945 I was given the Tzohar by a young Nazi soldier. I recognized it from its descriptions almost immediately, but it was many years before I really believed in its power.

Shortly after that Winter night, everything went to hell in Germany. The Allies were coming, and the war was all but lost. It took everything I had just to survive. The next few years were hard; I sold almost everything I had just to survive. But no matter how desperate I got, I could never part with the gem. One night when things were at their worst I sat in front of the fire holding it; staring at it. Then it happened—I saw my life. I saw everything. I saw my success in America. I saw the both of you. I know it sounds unbelievable, but it was true. The Tzohar showed me the path of my life, just as it did from the Angel Gabriel to Joseph. Many decisions I have made in my life—many that I know you do not agree with—come from the visions I saw that night.

After that I came to America, and you both know most of the story of my life here. In the 1980s I began hearing rumors in the art world that there were groups who believed that the Tzohar was a real gem and were searching for it. These weren't men of science and art, but criminals and terrorists. I began to fear that the Tzohar was too precious and too dangerous to keep in my possession. So, I hid it.

Which, my liebchens, brings me to the point of leading you here. I had always planned on retrieving the Tzohar and announcing its existence to the world so that all of mankind could revel in its glory and benefit from its power. But if you are reading this, I never got that opportunity, and in my dying moments I somehow did something to lead you here. I need you to fulfill my final life's work by bringing the Tzohar to the world.

Unfortunately, I cannot make this task easy for you, for I have no way of knowing with confidence who is reading this. The key to this safe deposit box may have somehow fallen into the wrong hands, and I cannot take the risk of the Tzohar being used for evil. So, this letter will lead you to the first of several clues that will lead you on the path…they are clues that only the two of you would be able to follow together.

I've included some monetary support to help you in this endeavor, as it will not be a cheap or easy undertaking. I ask one other thing of you, please take care of each other; remember how much you meant to me; and forgive me for bringing this into your life.

I love you both.

Chapter Sixteen

Noah Dew sat in the rented SUV in a parking lot across from the Melrose Hotel. He was in a good location; he had a good view of the main entrance of the hotel, but he could not be easily seen himself. He rubbed his eyes, and attempted to shake away the mind numbing boredom. He was amazed at how tiring it was just to sit in one spot—watching and waiting.

He had been sitting here for hours. He was furious with himself for losing them when he was attempting to follow them this morning. Dallas rush hour traffic was too congested, and he was not used to driving in a city this size. He was not a professional when it came to surveillance and reconnaissance, and he was afraid he had demonstrated that this morning. He thought for a moment about how disappointed his father would be in him. Then, he quickly forced that thought from his mind.

Soon the old Nazi's boyfriend and the other man would be back, and he would put an end to this once and for all. If he had not been so intent in his purpose, he would have been repulsed by the thought of any contact with the two sodomites. They were an abomination before God, and even if they had not stolen the Holy Light, he would want to kill them anyway.

He was only thirty years old, but looked much older. His arms were covered with tattoos; all homemade and administered by his father, uncles, and brothers. His hair was shaved short, and he always carried a Bible with a worn leather cover in his back pocket.

He thought about getting out of the car to walk around the block and clear his head, but he resisted the urge. He was afraid he would miss the sodomites' return, and thus his chance to find the Holy Light. He watched as students at an elementary school down the street yell and squeal as they chased each other on the playground.

He was proud that he had never attended one day of public school among the unbelievers. His parents had home schooled him and his seven brothers and sisters, understanding that no one could impart the word of the Lord to them as well as they could.

He was raised in a very strict Christian sect; an offshoot of the Pentecostals in rural Tennessee. Their church was composed mostly of members of the Dew extended family. All of the members of the church lived close to one another on contiguous property which had been purchased by a common ancestor in the 1930s.

Until he was nearly twenty, Noah knew almost no one outside of the compound, and he still went out of his way to avoid outsiders. His father had always told him that the unbelievers had no desire but to persecute them; just as the Jews had done to Christ. That's why being in this city—this modern day Sodom and Gomorrah—was so unbearable.

Two policemen on Segways passed by Noah's parking place and seemed to look at him a little too intently for his comfort. He picked up a city street map of Dallas and pretended to be studying it carefully. They looked away and continued down the sidewalk.

Noah put the map back down on the car seat, and smirked as the cops rode away. He had very little use for the police; or really any kind of government *authority*. His uncle had been killed by ATF agents and Tennessee State Troopers in 1995. They had tried to take him in for questioning on what they said was unlawful weapon possession, but he had held up in his family's cabin and had defied them. He said he would not subject himself to the *law of man*, only to the *law of God*. After three days the agents had stormed the house (by saying that Noah's aunt and cousins were hostages) and murdered his uncle.

But that was not the first event that caused him to distrust the law of man. When Noah was a child, Tennessee Children's Services tried to have him and his brothers and sisters taken from the family after his Mama had died. She had been bitten by a rattlesnake during a serpent handling ceremony at a church service. Their services lasted for many hours at a time, but even after being bitten she refused to leave; she sat in a back pew, fading in an out of consciousness. She lingered for almost a day in agonizing pain before the Lord finally took her.

Noah had cried when his Mama died, but his Daddy had explained it was God's will. As it said in the Gospel of Mark: *And these signs shall follow them that believe: In my name shall they cast out devils; they shall speak with new tongues. They shall take up serpents; and if they drink any deadly thing, it shall not hurt them; they shall lay hands on the sick, and they shall recover.*

His Daddy explained that his Mama was not yet perfect in her belief of the Lord, and that God had taken her to Heaven so that he could perfect her faith. But, that she would be waiting for them in Heaven.

He wondered if his Daddy was with her now in Heaven. It had now been over five years since his father had been murdered by the Jew. A Jew, who like his father, had also been seeking the gem of Holy Light.

Neither the Jew nor his father had obtained the gem then, but Noah was certain that his father's murderer was still seeking it with every fiber of his being; just as he was today. However, Noah had an advantage the Jew did not have; the name—Zeffner. His father had mailed him the note from England the day before he was killed:

Noah—the Holy Light will soon be in our church's hand; guiding us to our destiny. The Jews and Muslims challenge me at every turn, but I know the name of the thief of the Gem—Zeffner.

That was all his father had written, but it was enough. He had researched the name "Zeffner" which had not proved to be difficult since the man had gained fame and fortune—undoubtedly through the bastardization of the Holy Light. He tracked this Zeffner throughout the history of his life; all the way back to when he was stealing art for Hitler. He researched and tracked his life after he moved to the United States in the early 1960s, and became well regarded—even famous—within his chosen field. He read all the articles that he could find written by the man, and watched every interview conducted with him. He could have blindly confronted him when he first learned of his existence, but Noah Dew found it important to be patient and understand this man first.

Always know your enemy, his daddy used to say.

Noah was certain that Rudolph Zeffner was the man who possessed the Gem of Holy Light. And, he was as close as Texas! His father had followed clues and scripture throughout the Holy Land and Europe for years in his search for the Holy Light. And, all along, it had been within a day's drive of his Tennessee church!

Noah had found the old Nazi sodomite, and when he realized that the Holy Light was not in his possession, he killed him. He killed him in the name of vengeance for the Lord.

In a way, he regretted acting on his impulse of hatred for the man. Again, he knew he would have disappointed his father that he let his base emotions get the best of him. But still, he knew somehow the old bastard would lead him to the gem; and so then he followed—and he waited.

Noah had waited his whole life for this; God will grant him the patience to wait a little longer.

Chapter Seventeen

After they finished reading the letter, Gabe put it, the money, and the business card back in the envelope. He used the phone on the table to call the bank employee to come and retrieve them from the viewing room. He followed the woman back into the vault where she placed the metal box back into the safe deposit box, and reinserted his key as she did the bank's master. The three of them took the elevator to the main lobby, and both Gabe and Kevin thanked her for her assistance.

They came out of the bank with the envelope still in hand, and walked the few blocks back to the rental car without saying a word to each other. They got into the car, Gabe started it, then they began to drive away.

"Wow," Kevin said finally.

"Yeah, wow is right."

"This is unbelievable—when Rudy was murdered I knew there was something bigger, but I had no idea it would be anything like this."

"Yeah," Gabe said. "But, the question is—what do we do about it now?"

"What do you mean what do we do now?" Kevin asked sharply. "We do what Rudy asked us too—we find this Tzohar thing."

"Really, Kevin? We're going to find a mysterious Biblical object that most likely only existed in myth, and give it to the world? Do you even know what the Tzohar is?"

"No. I don't know what it is, and I don't really care. What I do care about is that Rudy asked me to do this for him and I'm going to do it. This was his last—and really, only—request of me. That's a good enough reason for me. I'd think that would be good enough for you as well."

Gabe sighed, but did not reply. They continued to ride in silence for several minutes, until Gabe finally spoke.

"Ok, you and Rudy win. We'll find the mystical artifact that hasn't been seen in thousands of years and hand it over to the Smithsonian or something."

Kevin smiled at him.

"See, when you say it like that it doesn't sound so hard, does it?"

Gabe tried unsuccessfully to stifle a laugh.

"I don't know why this surprises me—that man always did love making me jump through hoops," he said. "But, if we're going to do this we need to come up with some kind of plan."

"Ok, what do we do first?"

"We have a drink."

✳ ✳ ✳ ✳

Gabe and Kevin ended up at a small bar in Oak Lawn. It was only early afternoon, but Gabe found himself in dire need of a cocktail. Some conversations seemed to require a drink; and this was definitely one of them.

"So," Kevin asked. "Do you know what this Tzohar thing is?"

"Yes, actually I do," Gabe replied. "In fact, I wanted to write my doctoral dissertation on it, but Rudy of all people talked me out it. He said it was a ridiculous topic."

"Really? He said it was ridiculous, but he set all this up just to get us to search for it?"

"Yeah," Gabe said with a slight smile. "Seems kind of ironic doesn't it? But, to be honest, it seems to make a lot more sense now."

"What do you mean?"

"I could never understand why he was so dismissive of the topic, because—not to sound conceited—I thought it was brilliant. But I listened to him, and I ended up writing my dissertation on religious iconography of the Incas. I wowed my committee and got awarded my PhD with flying colors. I just chalked it up to Rudy once again knowing better than I did."

"And, now?"

"Now? Now I think he was afraid of me getting too close

to something he wasn't ready for me to know."

Kevin sat for a moment and considered what Gabe had said.

"So, what is the Tzohar?"

"Well, you were a good Catholic boy, right?"

"Yep, Saint Nicholas for kindergarten through eighth grade, and Bishop Bernard's for High School. I even considered going to Notre Dame for a while. Not to mention I was first in my confirmation class and an altar boy. My priest loved me."

"Yeah," Gabe said with a chuckle. "I'm sure he did."

Kevin tried to ignore the double entendre.

"So, altar boy, what are the opening lines of the Bible?"

Kevin quoted from memory. *"In the beginning God created the heaven and the earth. And the earth was without form, and void; and darkness was upon the face of the deep. And the Spirit of God moved upon the face of the waters. And God said, Let there be light: and there was light."*

"Wow," Gabe said. "Very impressive."

"First in my confirmation class, remember?"

"Ok, so what was the light?"

Kevin looked at him with surprise.

"Well, it was the sun—wasn't it?"

"Nope," Gabe said confidently. "According to Genesis 1, verses 14 through 19, the sun, moon, and stars weren't created until the fourth day."

"So, then—what was the light on the first day?"

"That, Kevin—that was the Tzohar."

Chapter Eighteen

Kevin looked at Gabe with what could only be described as wide-eyed amazement.

"So, you're telling me that we're going to search for the light God created on the first day?" he asked.

"Well, not exactly," Gabe explained. "The Tzohar was the result of the light, but the first light—also called the primordial light—was something different. Interestingly, scientists call the oldest light in the universe—light believed to be left over from the 'big bang' as primordial light. I've always found it fascinating how science and religion can overlap."

"Yeah," Kevin said impatiently. "Real fascinating. So, what exactly are we trying to find? If not God's original light—what then?"

"According to the book of Genesis, the primordial light was so bright that it was possible for Adam to see from one end of the world to the other. But, when Adam and Eve ate of the forbidden fruit, God punished them by taking away the light. God then trapped a small portion of that light into a glowing stone—*the Tzohar*—which the angel Raziel gave to Adam and Eve when they were expelled from the Garden of Eden to remind them of everything they had lost."

"Yep," Kevin said. "That Old Testament God didn't mess around when he was mad at you."

Gabe ignored him—Kevin had abandoned his altar boy upbringing a long time ago.

"But," Gabe continued. "The story doesn't end there. Adam passed the Tzohar to his son Seth who became a great prophet by staring into the stone. From there it passed from generation to generation, ending up with Methuselah who lived longer than anyone else by sleeping within its glowing light. A few generations later, it ended up with Noah…"

"*The* Noah—with the ark?" Kevin asked.

"The very same. In fact, Noah was told by God to hang the Tzohar on the deck, where it illuminated the ark for forty days and forty nights. That verse—Genesis 6:16—is actually the only place in the Bible where the Tzohar is referred to by name. And, even then, only in the original Hebrew. After that, it supposedly fell into the sea, and settled into a cave—the same cave where Abraham was born many years later and cared for by the Angel Gabriel. Gabriel placed the stone around Abraham's neck, and he grew from a baby to a man in thirteen days. Abraham wore the glowing stone around his neck for the rest of his life, and anyone who was sick and looked upon it was miraculously healed."

"The stone was handed down a few more times and went to Jacob, who gave it to his beloved son Joseph, along with the coat of many colors. When Joseph's brothers stripped him of his coat and threw him into the dark pit they didn't understand how precious the stone was and didn't take it from him. While in the dark pit filled with snakes and scorpions, the stone around Joseph's neck began to glow. At that point, the Angel Gabriel appeared to him and he was no longer in a pit—he was in Gabriel's palace. And, when Joseph looked out the window of the palace, he could see the full future of mankind revealed."

"So, the Angel Gabriel shows up in the story a few times?"

"Yes," Gabe answered. "That's originally what drew me to the topic. For obvious reasons, my namesake has always been of personal interest to me. And, I've always found it interesting how Gabriel was one of only three angels named in the Bible, but yet he played such a major role in Judaism, Christianity, and Islam. The Tzohar seemed to follow him around like a prop."

"After getting rescued from the well and being sold into slavery, Joseph fulfilled his destiny by becoming the King of Egypt. He kept the precious stone with him at all times, and it was eventually buried with him."

"So, the Tzohar ended up in Joseph's grave?"

"Not permanently. The Tzohar was retrieved from Joseph's coffin by Moses. Moses was told in a dream to take the glowing stone and hang it in the tabernacle. Which is the origin of the *Ner Tamid*—the eternal light which hangs over the ark in every synagogue in the world."

"*Moses?*" Kevin exclaimed. "That thing was owned by a regular who's who of the Bible wasn't it?"

"It certainly played a prominent role, yes. But, from there the story gets a little fuzzy. Rumored tales of the Tzohar surface during the life of Jesus, the Roman Empire, Europe in the Middle Ages, even in the early Mormon Church in America. If the legends are to be believed, there are groups of people who have been searching for the Tzohar since the time of Moses—and still seek it today."

"I've never heard any of this before. It's amazing that something with such a prominent role could keep such a low profile," Kevin said.

"Well, maybe you don't recognize the name, but most people are familiar with the concepts. After all, you've encountered an eternal light with every Catholic Church you've visited."

"You mean the Altar Lamp?"

"Exactly. Basically, the Christian appropriated version of the *Ner Tamid*. It doesn't stop there—you were a Boy Scout, right?"

"Yes, started as a Cub Scout, and was a Boy Scout until I was fifteen."

"Do you remember *The Light of Christ*, the Boy Scout medal given for religious service? A lot of scholars believe it has its roots in the Tzohar as well."

"That's quite an amazing story," Kevin said. "I really only have one question."

"Just one? What would that be?"

"The last known documented owner of the stone was Moses, right?"

"That's correct, according to the religious texts we have available."

"So," Kevin asked. "How exactly did this magical rock get from the presenter of the Ten Commandments to an old German gay man?"

Gabe smiled and shrugged his shoulders.

"I guess that's what he intended for us to find out."

Chapter Nineteen

Gabe glanced at his watch. It was almost 5:00 P.M. , and they had been sitting there in the bar discussing the Tzohar and Rudy's letter for nearly three hours. The time had gone by remarkably fast; despite the bizarre nature of the situation and everything else that had happened, it felt good being with Kevin again.

He immediately tried to push that thought from his head.

"So," Kevin said, breaking the uncomfortable lull in the conversation. "What about this first clue?"

Gabe reopened the envelope and pulled out Rudy's letter, and the small business card. He held the card in his hand, turning it over and feeling the raised text. It was approximately three inches by two, and printed on a good quality grey linen stock with deep red lettering. It was obviously professionally printed, which did not surprise him coming from Rudy. He read the text on the card out loud.

"The first path begins at the temple of eleven warriors—brave and bold."

"…Whose fame will ever stand," Kevin said as a response.

"What?" Gabe asked, surprised.

"'Eleven warriors brave and bold whose fame will ever stand.' It's from Ohio State's football fight song."

"A football fight song? That doesn't make any sense."

"Actually," Kevin said, rubbing his chin. "I think it makes a lot of sense. Rudy loved football—he always said it reminded him of a modern day version of the Roman gladiators."

He thought for a moment then added with a wink.

"I also think the tight pants didn't hurt."

Gabe thought about what Kevin said, and it really did make a lot of sense. He had forgotten what a huge fan of college football Rudy was. He had always thought it kind of odd; partially because of Rudy's background and lineage, but also because Gabe himself had never shared the interest. He just didn't seem like the typical football fan.

"Remember," Kevin continued. "He had an autographed photo of himself with every Ohio State football coach since Woody Hayes."

Gabe nodded in acknowledgement.

"So, this temple would be…"

"It would be Ohio Stadium. What else could be the temple of the eleven warriors, other than the football stadium?"

Kevin sat back and smiled, pleased with himself that *his knowledge* could contribute to the quest.

"So," Gabe said, throwing two twenties on the table to cover their bill. "I guess we're heading back to Columbus to search the stadium."

"We might not have to search too hard."

"Why is that?"

"They ran a fund-raising campaign a few years back where fans could buy engraved memory bricks that were placed around the stadium. Rudy bought one. I'm willing to bet that's a good place to start."

"You know, Kevin," Gabe said, standing up from the table. "I think I'm beginning to understand why Rudy said it would take both of us to solve this."

Chapter Twenty

Gabe and Kevin left the bar a few minutes later, and headed back to the Melrose in the rental car.

"I'll use the business center at the hotel to look for flights back to Columbus. Having my laptop stolen is a real pain."

"We can probably get something back in the morning," Kevin said. "It's been quite a day, and I'm exhausted. I can't imagine one extra day in the search for a glowing rock thousands of years old will make that much of a difference."

Gabe nodded in agreement.

As they pulled into the parking lot at the Melrose Hotel, Gabe's cell phone began to ring. He answered; it was Molly Newman.

"Gabe," she asked excitedly. "Where the hell are you?"

"We're in Dallas," He hesitated a moment before continuing. "Kevin and I wanted to check out first hand if we could find out any more information about Rudy."

He decided not to go into too much detail with Molly about the events of the day—finding the key in the jacket of Rudy's tux, or the contents of the safe deposit box. Partially because of the way she had reacted earlier to their story, but also because he suddenly realized he had no idea how to even begin to tell it.

"My sergeant says that the Dallas PD will want to talk

to Kevin," she said. "They want to question him about Zeffner's death."

"Why? He already told them what he suspected, and they acted like he was nuts. Do they think there might be something to the story now."

"Gabe," Molly said patiently. "You're not getting it. They suspect Kevin may have some involvement in the murder."

"What? Why?" Gabe asked angrily. "That's absurd—why would they think that?"

"Because, there were witnesses in their building that heard them arguing a few days before the murder," she paused for a moment, then added "Not to mention Kevin is the beneficiary of a pretty large life insurance policy."

"This is absolutely ridiculous," Gabe said sharply.

"I know, Gabe," Molly said quietly. "But sometimes people do things that you could never expect. If you really want to help Kevin, you should take him to the Dallas PD—give them a chance to get this straightened out."

Gabe's head was spinning—he could not believe what he was hearing.

"Ok, ok, sure," he said. "Thanks for calling."

"Gabe…" Molly began to say, but Gabe had already pressed the end call button.

Kevin looked at Gabe, confused by his reaction to the phone call.

"What was that about?"

"Kevin, I think things have just gotten a lot more complicated."

* * * *

Gabe pulled into a parking place, and repeated to Kevin the content of his conversation with Molly.

"Yes," Kevin said. "We had been arguing, but it isn't like it sounds. I had gotten an offer to go on tour playing with a show. Rudy thought I should do it, but I didn't think it was a good time to leave him alone."

"It could really be better described as a serious conversation, as opposed to an argument," he added. "Damn condo busy-bodies."

"Ok, ok," Gabe said. "But, that combined with the insurance policy has them asking some questions."

"I didn't know anything about there even being an insurance policy. I'm as surprised as anyone about that."

"Maybe we should go talk to them—just to get this all straightened out."

"Really?" Kevin asked angrily. "What are we going to explain? How we cut open a dead man's suit jacket—while he was wearing it no less—than took $150,000 out of his safe deposit box? Yeah, that's a brilliant idea."

"Kevin, try to calm down. We'll make them understand—we'll tell them about Rudy's letter and the clues he left for us—that will help explain it."

"Gabe, I may have bought the story about the five thousand year-old glowing rock owned by everyone from Adam to Moses, but what do you really think the police are going to say about that?"

Gabe was quiet, and thought about what Kevin was saying.

"Yeah," he said finally. "I guess you're right. We need to get to the bottom of this whole Tzohar thing. If we can do that, maybe we can find out who killed Rudy over it."

"Thank you," Kevin said. "Thank you for knowing that I couldn't have anything to do with this."

"Of course," Gabe said, squeezing Kevin's forearm. "But I think we need to go back to Columbus tonight—the sooner we get this resolved, the better."

✳ ✳ ✳ ✳

Gabe backed the car out of the parking space and pulled out onto Oak Lawn Avenue, and headed toward I-35 and DFW Airport.

Noah Dew started his car, and followed them out onto the street.

What were they doing? He was sure they were going back into the hotel, but then they suddenly left in the car again.

This time he would not lose them. He would follow them, and when he caught them they would have no choice but to lead him to the Holy Light.

Chapter Twenty One

They landed back in Columbus shortly after 7:00 the next morning. The direct flights between Dallas and Columbus were sold out, and the only flight they could get was a Northwest flight that connected through Minneapolis.

During the four hour layover, Gabe visited a sundry store to buy a toothbrush and some toothpaste. After sleeping on the plane during the flight from Dallas he felt like something had crawled into his mouth and died.

He had left his toothbrush, toothpaste, and a few other personal items at the Melrose Hotel. After the call from Molly, he and Kevin had been in such a hurry to get back to Columbus, they had abandoned the overnight bag he had brought with them in the hotel. It really was not that big of a loss; it was just a freebie duffle that he had gotten when he had bought some cologne. He was sure Calvin Klein and Macy's would not let him down for a replacement sometime in the future.

After arriving back at Port Columbus, Gabe and Kevin took the shuttle out to long term parking where Gabe had left his car. Gabe paid the Somali woman at the parking gate the twenty-four dollars he owed for the one-plus day of parking, and pulled out onto International Gateway heading toward the interstate.

"Do you want to go back to my place first, or just head straight over to campus?"

"Let's just get this over with," Kevin replied. "I might be able to enjoy a shower and a nap a lot more if I'm not worrying about an APB being out on me."

Gabe nodded silently, and pointed his car toward Interstate 71 and the campus of The Ohio State University. He had not spent much time on campus since his unceremonious dumping a few years ago, and he did not relish the idea of returning. Especially considering these circumstances.

Gabe parked his car in a visitor parking lot near the Fisher College of Business, and he and Kevin walked the few blocks to Ohio Stadium.

"I used to love coming to football games here," Kevin said.

"I've never actually been to a football game—here or anywhere else."

"How could you have been at Ohio State for that many years as a student and faculty and never go to a Buckeyes' game?"

"I guess it just never really interested me. I like the band though."

Gabe was not positive, but he was pretty sure that he saw Kevin roll his eyes at him. He smiled to himself; some things would never change.

They approached the stadium from the north side at the main entrance and rotunda. Kevin looked in both directions; not sure which direction to head.

"Any idea where this brick of Rudy's is?" Gabe asked.

"No, I've never seen it. But, they seem to go in both directions around the stadium," Kevin said, motioning toward the various imprinted bricks on the ground stretching out in front of them.

The engraved bricks were integrated into the walk-way and landscaping surrounding the stadium. The bricks were of various sizes, and contained messages of support and admiration for the Ohio State team. Fans had paid anywhere between five hundred and five thousand dollars for the honor. Gabe wondered at exactly what point this kind of thing graduated from fan worship into a full-fledged religion.

"Let's head in this direction," Kevin said.

They started walking to the right around the stadium, carefully reading each engraved brick they passed every few feet. It was a bright, warm October morning and the Ohio State campus buzzed with activity. There was something about the energy of a college campus in the Autumn that Gabe had always felt seemed almost spiritual. He missed that.

They were dodging a group of jogging ROTC students, when Gabe spotted the nine inch by nine inch engraved brick.

"Could this be it?" he asked Kevin.

"Certainly looks like it," he replied.

They both read the engraved brick silently:

Rudolph Zeffner
Playa del sol
Eat, Drink, be Merry!
de Garza
Go Bucks!

They finished reading and looked at each other at nearly the same time.

"So, got a quick answer for this clue too?" Gabe asked.

"Nope, this one doesn't make any sense to me at all."

Gabe pulled out a pen and a small notebook and wrote down the contents of the brick. He also took his cell phone and took several pictures of it. He assumed it was possible the clue was not in the text; but something about the brick itself.

"I'm not sure what else we can really do here," Gabe said.

"Let me see your pen for a second," Kevin said.

"Do you need some paper too?"

"Nope."

Gabe handed him the pen, and Kevin dropped to the ground. He tried to jam the pen between Rudy's brick and the adjoining blank one.

"What are you doing?" Gabe asked alarmed. "Someone is going to see you."

"Maybe the clue isn't the brick, but something under it."

Kevin continued prying at the brick until it was raised from the surrounding ground slightly, then used his fingers to dislodge it further. He pulled the brick away from the ground. There was nothing but ground underneath it.

"Well, it was a good thought."

Kevin replaced the brick, and stepped his foot on it hard to wedge it back into place.

"Let's go back to my place," Gabe said. "I could use a hot shower and a change of clothes. We'll be able to think clearer then and we can get started on this clue."

Kevin started to say something, but then stopped and nodded. He was exhausted too, and he knew neither one of them would be able to do much right now.

"Ok," he said.

They turned around and began walking back toward the car, just missing the ROTC group as they jogged past them on their next lap around the stadium.

Chapter Twenty Two

G abe and Kevin made the nearly ten minute drive back to Gabe's house in near silence. Neither one could really think of anything else to say, and the fatigue was getting the best of them.

"I'm going to drop you off at my house," Gabe said. "If we're going to be able to do any kind of research at all, I need a new computer."

Kevin simply nodded in agreement. Standing around a computer store while Gabe searched for his next laptop did not sound too appealing. Not when he could take a hot shower and maybe grab a few hours of sleep.

Gabe pulled his spare house key out of the glove compartment and handed it to Kevin.

"This will unlock the dead bolt and the door lock," he said. "The alarm code is 7272."

Gabe pulled up in front of his house and stopped the car to let Kevin out. Kevin got out of the passenger seat, and turned back toward Gabe through the open door.

"Are you sure you don't want me to go with you?" Kevin asked.

"No, that's ok. It's nice of you to ask, but I know you'd rather be back sitting in that airport for four hours instead of standing around waiting for me to buy a computer."

Kevin simply smiled at him and closed the door. Gabe still knew him pretty well.

Gabe pulled the car away from the curb, and tried to think of where the closest computer store would be. He decided that the Best Buy on the east side would be the fastest and most convenient. The faster he got this accomplished, the faster he could decompress for a while.

As he drove the car toward the highway he started to think about the latest clue. *Playa del sol.* That line kept going through his mind. *Playa del sol.* Literally translated from Spanish it meant "beach of the sun."

Gabe began associating words in his head; something he only did when he was particularly tired, but sometimes resulted in some good ideas. Beach. Water. Resort. Ocean. Coast.

Coast! That sounded familiar. *La costa del sol*—the coast of the sun. It was a resort area of Spain that Rudy had loved. It was the very first trip to Europe they had taken as a couple. In fact, it had been Gabe's first trip to Europe at all.

It had been years ago, but the memories were still pretty fresh. It had been an amazing experience. He had felt so sophisticated; so mature and international. He could not remember the name of the small fishing village where they had stayed, but it was a quaint seaside town right out of the Middle Ages. He could still see it in his mind.

They had eaten almost every night at a little tavern right on the main street facing the sea. Gabe had suggested a few times that they try some place different, but Rudy always insisted that they go there. He seemed to be acquainted with the proprietors and would speak with them at length. Gabe's own Spanish was only slightly above high school sophomore level at the time, and he missed most of the conversation. But, Rudy and his hosts had always seemed to enjoy them. What was the name of that place?

Gabe pulled the small notebook out of his pocket where he had written down the engraved text from the stadium brick. One line caught his eye:

Eat, Drink, be Merry! de Garza

The word Garza seemed so familiar. Then it all seemed to come back to him at once. The seaside village where they had stayed on La Costa del Sol was named Estepona, and the restaurant was called Beber Gayo. He remembered the lettering stenciled on the window in English, *Mora Garza, proprietor*. Suddenly, it felt as though it was all just days ago instead of nearly three decades.

That had to be it! The line "eat, drink, be merry" roughly translated to *beber gayo*. And, "de Garza" meant "of Garza"— as in *Mora Garza, proprietor*.

It all fit together too nicely not to be the answer. He was happy that he had followed Rudy's advice to continue to improve his Spanish over the years.

He did an abrupt U-turn in the middle of the street. An illegal act throughout the city of Columbus, but he needed to get back and tell Kevin what he had figured out right away. He hoped that Kevin had his passport with him and that it was up-to-date; he did not relish the idea of another side trip to Dallas.

He pulled up in the alley behind his house and parked behind his garage. As he walked around the garage into the yard, some strange movement through a back window caught his eye. He stepped behind a tree in the yard, and tried to get a better look into the house.

He could see Kevin standing toward the front of the house facing toward the back, but he was not alone. He could see someone facing Kevin with his back to Gabe's view through the window. He could see the expression on Kevin's face. He looked terrified.

"Oh, Jesus," Gabe said under his breath.

He was not sure what to do. He reached into his pocket for his cell phone, then realized that he had left it laying on the car seat. He was afraid he might be seen if he tried to go back to retrieve the phone. Instead, he decided that he had no choice but to try to help Kevin.

He slipped over to the cellar door underneath the back window and slowly pulled it open. The squeaking of the door hinges seemed unbelievably loud. He peeked up through the window, but luckily the intruder had not seemed to hear. He seemed to be too focused on Kevin.

Gabe slipped down the cellar stairs and into the dark and damp basement. The ceiling was low, and although Gabe was only of average height, he had to duck to clear his head. The basement had been hand dug at the time of the construction of the house and the floor was compressed dirt.

He made his way over to what looked like an old bureau, and opened the doors. This was one of the main reasons that Gabe had chosen this house, the secret stairwell that exited behind a moving bookcase in the study. Although it was most likely used for bootlegging during Prohibition, as a lifelong connoisseur of Scooby-Doo cartoons, Gabe just could not resist buying a house with a secret passage.

He quietly walked up the stairs and into the hidden hallway. He looked around him for some kind of weapon, but all he saw was a large pipe wrench, left over from a not so successful do-it-yourself plumbing project. He picked up the wrench and slowly pushed open the bookcase that doubled as a door. If his plan was accurate (and for he and Kevin's sake he was counting on it) he should be coming into the room right behind the intruder.

He came into the room and heard the man speaking in a heavy southern accent to Kevin.

"Just tell me where it is," he said. "That's all you have to do. You don't have to die like the old German."

Kevin saw Gabe emerge from the moving bookcase in front of him, but he gave no indication of it; not even his gaze betrayed him. Gabe was impressed with his self-control.

Gabe quietly snuck up behind the intruder, raised the heavy pipe wrench in his right arm and brought it slamming down against the back of the man's head. He collapsed into a heap onto the floor, and dropped the revolver he had been holding on Kevin.

Kevin sprung into action and kicked the gun away from the unconscious man.

"Oh, my God! He was going to kill me. How did you know to come back?"

"I didn't," Gabe said, his heart pounding in his chest. "It just happened to work out that way."

"Christ! What do we do now?"

"We need to get out of here," Gabe replied. "We don't know if this guy was alone, or if he has friends nearby. And, we've got a trip to take—I think I've figured out the next clue."

Kevin did not wait for any further explanation, and headed past Gabe toward the back door.

"Ok, I'm with you. Let's get out of here."

Gabe looked down at the unconscious man. He could not believe how crazy this whole thing had gotten. He needed to call Molly; to let her know that Rudy's killer was lying on his study floor. But, Kevin was right—there would be time for that once they were in the safety of the car. Right now, he had never felt quite so unsafe in his own house.

Chapter Twenty Three

Gabe and Kevin barely slowed down enough to open the back door as they bounded from the house. They both jumped off the back porch, not bothering with the time to navigate the five stairs that led to the ground.

"Where the hell is your car?" Kevin asked.

"It's around the corner from the garage in the alley."

They both continued to run at full speed, terrified to look back to see if the man might be following them. Gabe hit the unlock button on his key remote while still several feet away from the car so that the doors would be unlocked when they reached the relative safety of the vehicle.

"Who was that guy?" Gabe asked, as he fumbled getting the key into the car's ignition. The car engine roared to life and Gabe dropped it into drive, peeling out and throwing gravel from the alley in all directions.

"Well, he didn't exactly formally introduce himself, but he's obviously looking for the same thing we are."

Gabe's eyes grew wide as he looked at Kevin.

"Only," Kevin said. "He didn't call it the Tzohar—he kept calling it the *Holy Light*. But, I made the leap in logic and assumed we were all talking about the same thing."

"What did you tell him?"

"Well, I tried to act like I didn't know what he was talking about, but I'm sure he knew I was lying. He was waving the gun at me and saying all this crazy religious shit, but that's when you came out of the bookshelf…by the way, having a secret passage in your house is cool as hell."

Gabe ignored the last comment.

"How did he get into the house?"

Kevin looked at him sheepishly.

"I let him in. The front door knob was turning and I thought it was you—I thought you forgot something. I opened the door and he pushed his way in."

Gabe's driving had grown somewhat more restrained as he got further from the house, and the immediate adrenalin rush was subsiding. Still, his hands continued to shake.

"I've got to call Molly," Gabe said. "The man who probably killed Rudy is laying on my living room floor, and we've got to make sure they get him."

Gabe picked up his cell phone from the car's center console and selected Molly's name from his address book. The phone rang several times before it was answered.

"Officer Newman," the voice on the other end of the phone answered.

"Molly—it's Gabe. The man we think killed Rudy is laying on my living room floor—I hit him with a pipe wrench when he was holding a gun on Kevin."

The other end of the line was silent. For a moment, Gabe

feared his cellular service had dropped the call.

"Molly…?"

"Jesus, Gabe," the voice finally said. "Have you completely lost your senses? First you go flying off to Texas with the chief suspect in Zeffner's murder, then you don't go talk to the Dallas police like I asked you to. Now, you're telling me that you cold cocked some guy on the head who you think murdered your friend…"

"Molly, it's complicated…"

"And why in the world would you call me instead of calling 911?"

"Because I know you. And, I knew you would help me."

He heard a long frustrated sigh on the other side of the line.

"Where are you now?"

"We're in the car. As soon as I knocked the guy out, we took off out of the house. We were afraid he might have accomplices."

There was more silence on the phone.

"Molly, we found out some things in Dallas. I'm convinced more than ever about there being a bigger conspiracy here. Rudy left us a letter telling us about a very valuable historical art piece that he had hidden years ago. He knew he might be killed for it, and he has left us clues so that we can find it."

"Clues?" Molly said, her voice rising. "For Christ's sake Gabe this is the real world—not the *DaVinci Code*! Think about what you're saying."

"I know, but you've got to believe me—this is real."

"If that's the case, then you two need to turn over whatever so called evidence you have to the Dallas Police right now. This is their murder investigation."

"We don't have enough yet. Not only will they arrest Kevin for Rudy's murder, but they would probably throw us both in a mental institution for even telling this story. We need to get more proof."

"I've got two squad cars on the way to your house. I put it in as a suspected robbery in progress. I need you to drive yourselves straight to the station. I've done what I can to try to protect Kevin—*and you*—but you have to understand how suspicious you're both starting to look."

"I know," Gabe said. "But, we've got to follow this to the next step. We're going to have to leave town for a few days to follow Rudy's next clue."

"That's not a good idea, Gabe. Even if you're not crazy and this whole story is real, you're better off to let the authorities handle it. If Rudolph Zeffner really was killed over this, what makes you think you're going to have any better luck?"

"I don't know that we will," Gabe said quietly. "All I know is that someone I loved was murdered over this, and

I can't stop now."

"Gabe..."

"Thanks, for your help, Molly."

He clicked the button to end the call, then powered off the cell phone.

Chapter Twenty Four

A fter Gabe hung up the phone, he continued to drive although he was not quite sure to where. His mind was muddled with thoughts of what Molly had said, and the events of the last few days.

After several moments of silence, Kevin spoke up.

"So, I assume from the conversation Molly isn't exactly a big believer in Noah's glowing rock, huh?"

"We didn't exactly get that far."

"Yeah, I know," Kevin replied. "You said we would be going out of town for a few days following the next clue—planning on sharing that tidbit of information with me?"

"Oh, my God," Gabe said, turning to Kevin with newly remembered excitement. "With everything that happened, I completely forgot about it. That's why I came back to the house so soon—to tell you that I think I've figured out the next clue location."

Gabe proceeded to tell Kevin about the "playa del sol" line engraved on the stadium brick, and how that had reminded him of the Costa del Sol in Spain. He explained that the line "eat, drink, and be merry" roughly translated to Beber Gayo, which was the name of the tavern he and Rudy had frequented every night while they were in Estepona. Finally, the "de Garza" reference which meant "of Garza," and Mora Garza was the proprietor of Beber Gayo. It all fit together too well not to be the answer.

"Wow. I never would have put that together."

"Well, in all fairness—I was there."

"So was I."

"What?"

"Yeah," Kevin began to explain slowly, picking up on Gabe's reaction. "Rudy and I went to Estepona for our second anniversary. He said something about how he 'knew I was finally ready' or something like that."

Gabe looked down at the steering wheel. Once again he was immediately thrust back into the unwelcome role of the jilted lover. Once again he was reminded of how what he thought was a very special time between Rudy and him was really just another item off the checklist as far as Rudy was concerned.

"Personally," Kevin said, clearing his throat and feeling every nuance of the awkward moment. "I didn't really enjoy it at all. The town was pretty and everything, but about the only Spanish I know I picked up from Maria on Sesame Street…and I think Spanish food sucks."

Gabe nodded his head but said nothing. He was really tired of feeling like this.

"Do you have your passport?" Gabe asked suddenly, forcing a change in the conversation.

"Yeah, I do. I always keep it with me anymore."

"Ok, well it looks like we're going to need to take a little road trip to Spain."

"I'm sure that won't be an easy task out of Columbus. Dallas was one thing, but this isn't exactly an international hub."

"I don't think we should fly out of Columbus," Gabe said. "Based on what Molly said, it sounds like you and I both are quickly becoming the chief suspects in Rudy's murder."

"You? How could they suspect you? You weren't even in Dallas when Rudy was killed."

"No, but you came to Columbus to see me right after. Then we both went jetting down to Dallas. Maybe they believe you killed Rudy as part of some plot we had, and now we're going to live happily ever after on the insurance money. Let's face it—it could be quite the salacious story…a gay lovers triangle where the two younger paramours kill the older wealthy one. It could give Nancy Grace fodder for her show for months."

"I can't believe that all this is really happening," Kevin said, shaking his head.

"I also don't think I should contact Molly anymore. I don't want to get her anymore involved than she already is, and I don't want her to be in the situation of having to choose between getting into trouble to help us, or turning us in."

"So, if we don't fly, how exactly are we going to get to Spain? It's a pretty long boat ride."

"I just think we need to fly out of somewhere else—maybe Pittsburgh or Cincinnati. I have a feeling someone may be keeping an eye out for us at the Columbus airport. And after today, I'm talking about both the good guys and the bad guys."

Gabe pulled the car over and parallel parked on the street across from Schiller Park in the German Village neighborhood. He turned off the car's ignition, and turned his cell phone back on.

He called up Expedia's mobile site on the phone and did a few quick searches on flying out of either Cincinnati or Pittsburgh to Malaga, Spain. There was a 10:30 p.m. flight listed out of Pittsburgh via JFK that would get into Malaga the next morning. It is a little over a three-hour drive to Pittsburgh from Columbus, which would give them just enough time to make a quick shopping trip for some supplies and still get to the Pittsburgh airport in time.

"Ok, it looks like Pittsburgh will work out perfectly."

He pulled out his wallet and retrieved his credit card so that he could buy the tickets online.

"It's a shame that Rudy gave us all this cash to use on his little adventure and we can't use it over the Internet."

"Yeah, a Visa gift card would have been more practical in

this online world," Kevin said with a smile. "Remember that if you ever send two ex-boyfriends out on a treasure hunt."

As Gabe was completing the online transaction to purchase the two tickets to Malaga, a text message popped up on the cell phone's screen. It was from Molly.

No perp @ ur place. Trail of blood on floor leading out the back door. Gabe—this is nuts. GO TO THE POLICE.

Gabe sighed, and turned the phone off once again.

Chapter Twenty Five

Noah Dew sat in his parked car on the street several blocks from the house he had just escaped. His head pounded, and he was having a difficult time focusing his eyes to see anything more than blurry lights. Although he had never experienced one before, he was pretty sure that he had a concussion.

The last thing he remembered was holding the gun on the one named Kevin. He had looked so frightened—much more so than the old German had when he had pointed the same gun at him. He had tried to deny knowledge of the Holy Light, but Noah knew he was lying. He was sure that Kevin was only seconds away from revealing everything to him.

Then everything went dark. The next thing he knew he was waking up in a pool of his own blood with the sounds of sirens quickly approaching. Using every last bit of strength he had, he pulled himself up and hurried out the back of the house as he heard the police cars stopping in front.

He had no idea what had happened, but figured that the old Nazi's boyfriend's companion must have somehow snuck up on him. Although, he could not imagine how—surely he would have heard the back door opening.

He knew the man who owned the house was named Gabriel Patrick. He found it absolutely repugnant that this man could share the name of the Archangel who was so closely associated with the Holy Light that he sought. He knew his name from the laptop he had taken from his house after following the Nazi's boyfriend to Ohio.

In fact, he knew quite a bit about Gabriel Patrick. Apparently, the idiot had never heard of password protecting anything on his computer, so his entire life was pretty much an open book for Noah to sift through.

He also apparently had never heard of cleaning up his Internet history, because every site he frequented was right there with the "remember me" option checked. Even his bank account was as easy as a few keystrokes to get into. Shortly after getting into the computer the first time, Noah set up a notification with the bank to send an alert to his own cell phone each time Patrick's credit card was used. Noah knew of the trip they were making to Dallas seconds after he had purchased the tickets.

But, probably best of all was the mapping web site that he used to track the GPS coordinates of his cell phone. Why someone would set something like this up to track their own cell phone location was beyond him, but he certainly was glad Patrick had. As long as the cell phone was on, Noah could know their location within a few feet anywhere in the world.

He had no idea where they were right this minute, but he

was sure as soon as he could get back to the computer they would announce it to him soon enough. Yes, the Lord was certainly looking out for him in this quest.

Right now, however, he needed to get some ice on his head. His head throbbed and he was feeling very sleepy, but he was trying his hardest to fight the urge to lay down on the car seat and close his eyes for a few minutes. If his head injury was as bad as he feared, he was afraid he might never wake up.

Gabe and Kevin arrived at the Pittsburgh airport at a few minutes before 9:00 P.M. On the drive from Columbus they had stopped at the Ohio Valley Mall on the West Virginia border to buy some clothes, luggage, and other supplies for their trip.

Gabe also used the opportunity to visit the mall's only electronic store to finally purchase a new laptop. Given a better selection, it probably was not the brand or model he would have chosen, but it was good enough for now. He was tried of being frustrated by the limitations of cell phone Internet access.

They boarded the plane at 10:00 for an on time 10:30 departure. From there it was a fifty minute flight to New

York, then seven more hours to Malaga.

Within minutes of boarding the flight, and before the flight safety instructions were given, both Gabe and Kevin were deeply asleep.

Chapter Twenty Six

The Iberian Airlines flight touched down in Malaga, Spain shortly after 8:30 A.M. local time. Despite the long flight time from New York, the trip had been somewhat pleasant. When purchasing the tickets Gabe had splurged for business class, and both he and Kevin had slept most of the flight. Gabe woke up just as the captain was announcing their incoming approach, and he felt surprisingly rested. Not bad for an airline seat.

Malaga is considered the heart of the Costa del Sol tourist region. It is a city with a population of over half a million people, and the fifth largest in Spain. Besides the beautiful beaches and glittering resort hotels, its main claim to fame is that Malaga was the birthplace of Pablo Picasso.

Their journey through Spanish Customs was fairly quick since they had checked no luggage; everything brought for the trip easily fit within the carry-ons they purchased on the drive to Pittsburgh. They handed the customs agent their properly completed forms and passports. The agent studied the documents, then glanced at Gabe and Kevin. He stamped the passports and waved them through. That was one of the advantages of visiting one of Europe's major tourist destinations; they were used to getting large numbers of people through customs without too much inconvenience.

It also gave Gabe some hope that Interpol obviously had not yet been contacted to begin looking for them.

Once in the main terminal of the Malaga Airport, their first stop was at *el cambio*—the currency exchange. They converted $10,000 of the cash Rudy had given them into Euros. That should be enough to cover whatever they would need to do for at least a few days.

Next, they headed straight for the transportation information desk to determine the best means to get to Estepona. It was around 80 kilometers from the airport to their destination; or a little over an hour's drive.

Gabe quickly decided against trying to rent a car. His International Driver's Permit was no longer valid, and the decision to make the trip was so rushed he had not had time to renew it. Besides, he absolutely detested driving in Europe—street signs and directional aids seemed to be purely an American luxury.

They found a taxi cab company that would take them to Estepona for 130 Euros. While that seemed a little pricey, it would be the cheapest and most efficient way of getting there. The taxi driver asked them for the address where they wanted to go in Estepona.

Gabe stopped for a moment—he had not considered the question before now.

"You know, I'm not exactly sure."

The taxi driver looked at him somewhat surprised by the response, but said nothing else. He popped open the trunk of the Volkswagen Scirocco that would serve as their transport to Estepona. Gabe and Kevin tossed their limited luggage into the trunk and climbed into the car's back seat.

The taxi driver took the coastal road out of Malaga. Gabe found it hard not to be amazed by the scenery. To his left all he could see was the blue brilliance of the Mediterranean, to the right was the rocky heights of the Sierra Bermeja mountains. As they passed the ruins of a crumbling castle dating back at least a thousand years, Gabe could not help but be impressed with the history of this land. Spain had been ruled by everyone from the Greeks, to the Romans, to the Arabs, to a military dictator—and up to and including the popular constitutional monarchy that rules today. At one time Spain had been the most powerful nation on earth, and the rest of the world had trembled as it spread the Inquisition from its shores.

Gabe could not help but remember the first time he had been here with Rudy. Not only had it been his first trip to Spain, but the first time he had ventured outside of the United States. He could remember how he felt then—so mature and so sophisticated. His life and future seemed truly limitless. So many things had changed since then.

The drive to Estepona took a little less than an hour.

Lacking an address to give the taxi driver, Gabe decided to have him let them off at the tourist office. Located near the center of the old village, he figured it was as good a spot as any to begin. Plus, they would have maps, and most likely friendly agents who could help them locate Mora Garza. Gabe knew he would know Beber Gayo when he saw it; but the problem was finding it.

The taxi driver dropped them off in front of the tourist office located at the junction of Avenida Juan Carlos and the sea front promenade. Gabe handed him two hundred Euro and told him to keep the change. It was the first time Gabe had seen the man smile since they had encountered him at the Malaga Airport.

"*Muchas Gracias senor,*" he said with a tip of his cap. "*Bienvenidos a España.*"

Gabe returned the smile and he and Kevin pulled their sparse collection of luggage from the cab as the driver pulled away.

Gabe tried the front door of the tourist office only to find it locked. It was nearly noon, and Gabe figured the office must be closed for lunch. He had forgotten about how most businesses tend to close down for several hours in the middle of the day. While usually he would find such an homage to age old tradition and culture charming; right now, however, he just found it inconvenient.

"So, now where do we start? Kevin asked.

"Do you remember which direction to Beber Gayo? You've been here since I have."

Gabe realized that his last comment had come out more pointed than he had intended. While the idea that Rudy had also brought Kevin to Estepona really bothered him, now was not the time to open these wounds.

"Sorry," Gabe said. "That didn't come out quite the way it was intended. But, do you remember?"

"I remember it was on the ocean. To be honest, I was sick pretty much the whole time we were here. The food—remember—it's all pretty much a blur now."

Gabe nodded in acknowledgement. As much as it pained him, he could not remember either. It was odd how a time and place he thought he could never forget seemed so distant and vague now.

"Yeah, I agree it was on the water. Let's just walk down the street facing the beach to see if anything looks familiar."

They turned right on Avenida de Espana which fronted the expansive city beaches of Estepona. The sun was bright, and the sky a brilliant blue that nearly blended into the Mediterranean. And, despite being mid-October it felt as hot as the middle of Summer. Gabe could understand why this area was Disney's original choice for the location of Euro Disneyland. It was truly a tourist's delight.

As they walked they passed tapas bars, seafood restaurants, small boutiques selling local goods, and calamari vendors manning small carts about every ten feet. They were approaching the marina and the end of Avenida de Espana, and Gabe was just ready to suggest that they turn around and try the other direction when he saw it—a small whitewashed building with a fading purple and teal awning. The small sign next to the door read:

Beber Gayo
Mora Garza, Proprietor

"Bingo," Gabe said.

Gabe pulled on the door handle of Beber Gayo, fully expecting to find that door locked as well. However, to his pleasant surprise the door opened freely. Some small bells hanging from the frame announced their arrival.

A young girl with long dark hair was standing behind the ornate bar, drying glasses. She looked at them and smiled broadly. She looked to be no older than eighteen.

"Buenos tardes," she said cheerfully.

"Buenos tardes," Gabe returned.

He introduced himself and Kevin, and told the girl that they were looking for Mora Garza, and wondered if she might be available.

"Mi abuela?" the girl asked. Obviously, she was Mora Garza's granddaughter.

The girl asked them to wait for a moment, and she disappeared into a doorway at the back of the restaurant's dining room. Kevin looked at Gabe and smiled.

"Your Spanish is really good," he said.

"Thanks, no one will mistake me for a native, but I guess I get by."

"I never had the skill or patience to pick up another language, although Rudy was always insisting I should."

The door reopened at the back of the dining room, and an older woman appeared in the doorway. If this was the same woman Gabe had met many years ago, she certainly looked a lot older than he remembered. She walked toward Gabe and Kevin, and eyed them suspiciously.

"You want Mora Garza?" she asked in English.

"Yes, ma'am," Gabe replied. "We're searching for her on behalf of a mutual friend—Rudolph Zeffner."

Gabe saw the woman's eyes grow wider, and her demeanor change. Gabe was not sure if the change was for the good or for the bad.

"I am Mora Garza. You say that you were sent by Rudolph, but I must be sure," she said. She squinted and looked hard at both Gabe and Kevin. "I do think you boys look familiar. But, Rudolph introduced me to a lot of boys over the years." She said the last sentence with a lilt in her voice.

"Señora Garza, we're seeking an art object on behalf of Rudolph. He gave us some information that led us to believe you may be able to help us." Gabe decided not to mention yet about Rudolph's murder. The woman seemed old and frail, and he did not want to upset her too much.

"So, you say," she said suspiciously. "Rudolph also tell me that men may come saying they come to me on his behalf, but they are lying. So, I ask you something that only a real friend of Rudolph would know." She stopped, and studied their faces carefully as she asked. "What is his favorite painting?"

Gabe and Kevin looked at each other, surprised by the question, but neither one hesitated to answer.

"His favorite painting is the *Village Street*," Gabe said.

"By Franz von Lenbach," Kevin added, and practically finishing Gabe's sentence.

Mora Garza looked at them, and tears welled up in her eyes. She reach forward, and squeezed both of them on their upper arms.

"So," she said, a tear escaping her eye and rolling down her cheek. "My Rudolph is dead."

Chapter Twenty Seven

Noah Dew had done everything to avoid sleep. On his way back from Gabe's house he stopped at McDonalds and bought four large cups of coffee. He downed them one right after another on the ten minute drive back to his motel.

He had sat in the car a few blocks from Gabe's waiting for his headache and dizziness to subside. After about twenty minutes he began to worry that he might look suspicious sitting in his car—holding his head—staring at nothing on the residential street.

Once he got back to his room it was all he could do to keep his eyes open. He lay down on his bed and closed his eyes. As he was fading off into sleep, he had brief thoughts that if he did die from his head injury at least it would be God's will. And, like so many times throughout his life, he left it all up to God.

He was not sure how long he had slept, but he was vaguely aware of it going from daylight to night, to daylight, and back to night again. He woke up with the driest mouth of his life, and to the beeping tones from Gabriel Patrick's computer. He pulled himself from the bed and stumbled over to the computer. He was briefly surprised for a moment that he had not died in his sleep.

He did not know how long the alarm had been going off

on the computer, but it indicated several new e-mails had been received in his in box. One of the e-mail messages caught his eye—it was a flight purchase receipt from Iberian airlines. Patrick had purchased two one-way business class tickets from Pittsburgh to Malaga, Spain.

Spain? Why would they have gone to Spain? Of course, he knew the answer—it must have something to do with the Holy Light. Somehow the old Nazi had told them where to find it, or even worse—had somehow given it to them and directed them to dispose of it.

He slammed his fists down on the cheap plywood motel desk. This was unbearable, and he cursed his own weakness. He should have been able to stop the sodomites, and obtain the Holy Light. His faith in the Lord must not be strong enough—that was the only reason he could contemplate for his failure. When he encountered them again he would kill them both with his own bare hands. The Lord *would* give him the strength to do that.

His entire life had been focused on finding and possessing the Holy Light. It had been the same with his father, and his father before him. In fact, it was the entire purpose and guiding principal of their church.

The Millfield Valley Holiness Church was founded in 1933 by Thomas Dew, Noah's grandfather. The elder Dew had ended up in southern rural Tennessee by way of New

Jersey. He had left home searching for work in the depths of the Great Depression. He found a job working the tobacco fields in Millfield Valley, and having run out of money to travel any further, he decided to stay. The rural countryside, and southern culture was completely foreign to his New Jersey childhood, growing up in the shadow of the New York City skyline.

One afternoon in late May of 1932, Thomas Dew was working in one of the fields near the northern edge of the county when a sudden thunderstorm approached. The storm came up so quickly that he had no time to take cover. As the storm raged around him, Thomas lay on the ground with his arms over his head, trying to protect himself from the wind, pounding rain, and hail. Suddenly there was a bright flash of yellow light, a deafening boom, then everything went black.

Thomas Dew woke up three days later having survived what was described as a nearly direct lightening hit. When he awoke, he told his caretakers a strange tale of being visited by God, who told him that he was destined to lead a church that would be devoted to his word, and which would dedicate itself to obtaining the Gem of Holy Light.

Dew explained to those around him that the Gem of Holy Light had been cast from the original light God created when the World began. Whoever possessed it would truly understand the word of God, and would have insight into all the mysteries of the universe. He told everyone that would listen that he was devoting his life to finding this gem.

Thomas Dew had grown up one of the few Protestants in a mostly Jewish neighborhood. While he or his family had never attended a synagogue themselves, he undoubtedly was exposed to many tenants of the religion. From his friends at school, to the conversations he overheard with the old women in the local market. It never occurred to him that his conversation with God may have actually been recalled memories of stories he heard of a Jewish relic called the Tzohar. He believed that he had been visited by God, and that it was his destiny to possess the Gem of Holy Light.

After being released from the hospital, he discovered that he was very different from the man he once had been. For one thing, he was no longer right handed; his dominant hand was now his left. His memory also dramatically improved; he had never read the entire Bible in his life, but he did so shortly after the strike. To his amazement, he discovered that he had memorized nearly the entire book.

He began telling the people in town about the changes that were occurring with him. Most listened politely, but many assumed the lightning strike had affected him mentally. One day he was in town when a little boy was hit by a car. Thomas was one of the first at the boy's side; he placed his hands on his head and told him that the Lord would take care of him. Dew knelt beside the boy, while others stood back in a circle around them; convinced that the boy's injuries were too severe to survive.

However, the boy did survive. And when he awoke from the coma, he told everyone how he had seen God when Thomas Dew had touched him; and God had told him to follow this man, for he was the messenger of the Lord.

Word spread quickly around the area about the miracle that had occurred, and the man who had been struck by lightning, survived, and spoken to God. Soon, people were coming from miles around to speak with Thomas Dew and to have him lay hands upon them. More and more people continued to seek him out until there were too many to see one at a time, so he began to hold services. That was the beginning of the Millfield Valley Holiness Church.

The church thrived over the next several years, growing to around one hundred members. Thomas Dew married a fifteen year-old local girl, and they had eight children; one of whom was Noah's father. While the church grew, the message that Thomas Dew preached remained the same—their destiny was to possess the Gem of Holy Light. He and the elders of the church intently researched the gem; determining what they sought was called the Tzohar in Jewish lore. Although, the elder Dew forbade anyone from ever referring to it by its Jewish name.

The church organized pilgrimages to the Holy Land and to Europe seeking the lost gem. The most important and respected men in the church were referred to as *the seekers*, and they were regularly dispatched by Thomas Dew to follow new leads on the whereabouts of their treasure. (A woman could never be considered worthy or suitable of being a seeker.)

When Thomas Dew died in 1988, his oldest son (Noah's uncle) became the new leader of the church, and Noah's father became the chief seeker. The church continued to become more guarded and isolated from regular society; most people in the nearby towns referred to it as a cult, and rumors spread about their strange ways and stashes of weapons. Local law enforcement, then later the FBI and ATF started to become interested in what might actually be happening on the church's forty acre compound.

The agencies' interest in the Millfield Valley Holiness Church is what led to the confrontation that ended in the death of Noah's uncle—the youngest son of Thomas Dew. Life within the church compound changed significantly after that. While the members of the church had once maintained polite coexistence with the local residents, after the confrontation with the FBI, every outsider became a potential enemy. The church became more and more isolated from mainstream society.

But that all seemed like a very long time ago to Noah Dew now. The only thing that continued to matter was that he would find the Gem of Holy Light and fulfill the destiny of his father and grandfather. He would do it in vengeance of his father's death, who was murdered by a Jew who also sought the gem.

Noah launched the GPS tracking web site that was linked to Gabriel Patrick's cell phone. It took a few moments to isolate his location, but quickly found Patrick in a small town on the southern coast of Spain called Estepona. From his careful surveillance of the life of Rudolph Zeffner, he knew that the old German had traveled to Estepona many times over the years. It was one of several locations that he frequented.

Dew pulled up the Orbitz web site to search for available flights to Estepona. Flying out of Columbus it would take him over thirty-six hours to get there—that may be too late. He remembered the tickets were purchased in Pittsburgh, so he checked PIT as the departure city. Still, he would take him nearly a day to get there.

He decided to wait and bide his time. With the GPS tracking site he could keep an eye on their location, and he could intercede if necessary. Besides—they would have to come back at some point. And when they did, he would be waiting.

Chapter Twenty Eight

TEL AVIV, ISRAEL

Namir Yosef looked up from his computer monitor as the younger man approached him.

"Sir," the younger man said. "We have information that Patrick and Hurst have traveled to Malaga, Spain."

"Spain? Well, that would fit one of the theories proposed," Yosef said.

"Really, sir? It has been proposed that the relic may have been taken to Spain?"

"Yes, that has been considered as one of many possibilities. My guess would be that they're heading to Estepona. Zeffner made many trips there over the years."

The younger man seemed very interested. "Do you believe that Spain is the location, sir?"

"After years of keeping an eye on Rudolph Zeffner, I'm not sure exactly what I really do believe. The man could keep you guessing, I'll say that for him."

The younger man nodded and said nothing. He had only been on this assignment for a few months, and he desperately wanted to impress his superior. He continued to stand in front of his desk, waiting for some additional acknowledgement.

"Thank you, Anon," Yosef said, attempting to dismiss his

underling as politely as possible.

The younger man's face flushed slightly as he thanked the man and walked away. Yosef turned back to his work on the computer screen.

He had been recruited by the Mossad nearly as soon as he graduated from the university, and had spent his entire adult career in service to the organization. For the past ten years he had been part of a task force that was responsible for what the agency referred to as "special considerations." One of those special considerations was the Tzohar.

Membership within the Mossad is considered very prestigious within Israeli society. It is well known as the government's institute for intelligence and special operations. However, what most Israeli's did not know was about its interests in other aspects of the Jewish faith and life.

The Mossad enjoyed a rich and honored history within the Jewish world. It was founded in 1938 as Mossad Le'aliyah Bet—ten years before Israel itself was a country. It started as a small Zionist organization whose mission was to bring Jews to Israel. Or, as it was known then—the British Mandate of Palestine.

While the Mossad was originally created to subvert the British quotas on Jewish immigration, its modes of operation, its ideology, and politics resulted in the creation of the intelligence agency for the Israeli government once it was established in 1948. What had once been an underground political operation during British rule, became an important part of the new country's establishment.

The Tzohar had been part of the special considerations unit for virtually its entire existence. The early leadership of the Mossad firmly believed that it was a genuine article—not some sort of Biblical myth. They had known for years that the relic was in the possession of the former Nazi art collector; they had even pinpointed the exact date he had received it. (Not to mention, had tracked most of its five thousand year history prior to that.)

The Mossad had concluded that a German national, Rudolph Zeffner, was in possession of the Tzohar in the early 1960s. There was some debate how the agency should proceed with that information. It was repulsive to most that a former Nazi would have possession of one of the most sacred religious artifacts of Judaism. However, before there was any resolution determined, Zeffner had moved to the United States. While the Mossad was not necessarily against running such an operation on American soil, the government at the time thought it was too risky. After all, they calculated that the Tzohar had been in his possession for nearly twenty years at that point. Obviously, if he had any public intentions with the relic why wouldn't he have done it long before then?

So, despite the Mossad's objections, the Israeli government had made the decision that no action would be made to forcibly retrieve the Tzohar from Zeffner—particularly while he continued to live in America. However, by the late 1960s Zeffner had become a full fledged citizen of the United States which made it even more unlikely for the government to allow such a mission. Besides, by that time the Israeli government was much more preoccupied with the Egyptians.

So, for the past four-plus decades the Mossad had continued to carefully watch Zeffner from a distance. For nearly a quarter of that time, Namir Yosef had been the agent in charge of the operation.

The task force frequently picked up chatter through a variety of sources that told them that the Tzohar was still actively sought by a variety of groups. At different points over the past forty years, groups ranging from the Russian mafia to the Vatican had launched initiatives to try to discover its existence and location. Very few of them ever made it beyond the chatter stage; and the only groups which had maintained an active quest over the years had been multiple groups of Muslims, a small sect of ultra-fundamentalist Jews, and a few far-right Christian groups within the United States and Europe.

Yosef had always been impressed with the way Rudolph Zeffner had stayed below the radar. In the chatter that the Mossad monitored, Zeffner's name had never been mentioned as a possible possessor of the Tzohar. And, the old German never did anything to suggest that he had any link at all to it. This was a man who was one of the foremost experts in the world on religious art, yet he himself never mentioned the Tzohar—one of the greatest religious relics of all time—in any of his writings or public speeches. In the few occurrences over the years when he had been asked about the possibility of the Tzohar's existence, he inevitably laughed it off as simply a relic of myth—after all, he only bothered himself with real art that actually existed.

The Mossad's official policy on the Tzohar was simply one of protection and containment. Their desire was for it to only keep its current mythical reputation, and be safely locked away somewhere. Yosef often thought that Zeffner made this part of his job very easy. That was, until last week. Now, the comfortable status quo had been disrupted.

Zeffner's murder had come to the Mossad's attention nearly as quickly as it had to the Dallas police department's. Originally, the Dallas police assumed that this was simply the home invasion and robbery of an upscale condo gone horribly wrong. Now, the police was focusing the investigation on Kevin Hurst, Zeffner's current young boyfriend on the misguided motive of life insurance money. Over the years, Yosef had come to know nearly as much about the revolving young men in Zeffner's life as he did Zeffner himself. However, from the Mossad's best knowledge, Zeffner had never told any of his *companions* about the existence of the Tzohar.

The Mossad was certain that the truth had finally caught up with Rudolph Zeffner, and he had been murdered by one of the groups or individuals who sought the Tzohar. Namir Yosef was not entirely sure which group it was, but his personal money was on the Muslims or the Christians, since the prime Jewish suspects had not left Israel in the last several weeks.

Yosef was relatively sure that whoever had killed Zeffner had not gotten the Tzohar. For no other reason than the old man was too smart to have kept the relic with him. The strange behavior of Kevin Hurst and Gabriel Patrick—another former lover of Zeffner—made him especially sure that the Tzohar was still hidden and safe. At least, for the time being.

The Mossad had been covertly tracking Hurst and Patrick since the younger man had suddenly taken off from Dallas to Columbus in the few hours after Zeffner's murder. Yosef believed that Zeffner must have somehow tipped off the men about the Tzohar, and they were seeking it at his direction. He had no idea what sort of message the old man could have left; however, he had learned over the years not to underestimate Rudolph Zeffner.

The two men were clearly not spy material; not only

were they unaware of the Mossad tracking them, but they also did not seem to be aware of the attention of either the Muslim extremist cell or the fundamentalist Christian who was watching them as well. Right now, everyone just seemed to be hanging back and waiting for the men to lead them to the Tzohar.

The Mossad was content to play the waiting game as well. After all, that had essentially been the *modus operandi* for the past forty-plus years. However, Namir Yosef knew the relative calm would not last. At some point in the near future this entire situation would finally come to a head, and the Mossad would need to be in place to secure the Tzohar. Yosef had no doubt that this event would require the spilling of blood, but in a mission this serious he would have absolutely no qualms about doing so.

Chapter Twenty Nine

Mora Garza approached the table where Gabe and Kevin sat.

"Rudolph had said that you boys would come one day looking for this," she said, in near perfect English.

She carried with her a small wooden box which she sat on top of the table where Gabe and Kevin sat.

"He gave this to me to keep for him a few years ago. As usual, I thought he was just being overly dramatic, but there was something that told me this was very important to him."

Gabe smiled at her thoughtfully. "Senora Garza, did you know Rudy for a long time?"

"Oh, yes, oh yes," she said smiling. "I first met Rudolph in 1947. He had come to Spain to get away from the hardships of Germany after the war. He spent a lot of time in Spain before he moved to America."

"I knew he had vacationed in Spain quite a bit, but I had no idea that he had spent that much time here," Gabe said.

"Well, I'm sure there is a lot about Rudolph that would surprise you," Mora Garza said. "He lived a very interesting life."

Both Gabe and Kevin nodded their heads in silent agreement. It did not really surprise either one of them to hear that there was a lot more to Rudy's life than they probably knew.

"How did Rudolph die?"

Kevin and Gabe looked at each other uncomfortably before either spoke.

"He was murdered, Senora Garza," Gabe finally said.

Her eyes grew wide. "Murdered?" she whispered hoarsely. "How could anyone murder my Rudolph?"

"We're not sure, ma'am," Kevin said. "The police think that it may have been a home invasion and robbery." He decided not to mention his recent ascension to the top of the suspects list.

Mora Garza sat at the table with her head in her hands and she cried softly.

"But, Kevin and I think there may be more to it than that. Rudy left us a message—a message that led us here to you."

Mora Garza looked up at Gabe, wiped a tear from her eye, and smiled sadly.

"Yes," she said. "And, he knew he could trust me to keep what he wanted you to have." She nudged the wooden box toward Gabe. "I never asked him what it was—I trusted him enough not to ask."

She stood up from the table. "I'll leave you boys alone with the package that Rudolph left for you."

"Senora Garza," Kevin said. "You're more than welcome to stay. I'm sure Rudy would have wanted you to know what was in the box as well. He obviously trusted you very much."

"Thank you, Kevin. But, no. I never asked Rudolph about certain things, and he never told me certain things. Maybe he was protecting me, or maybe he just thought they were things I shouldn't know. Either way, I'd rather keep things the way they are." She turned and walked back into the kitchen.

Gabe looked around the empty dining room at *Beber Gayo*. It was the middle of the afternoon, and the town streets were quiet. It was the height of siesta hours. There seemed to be no concern about anyone overhearing them, or seeing what was in the mystery box Rudy had left for them.

Kevin picked up a butter knife off the table and jammed it into the small space between the wooden lid and side of the box. He pried it upward, pulling the nails which held the lid in place from the box structure. He pulled the lid away, and pushed aside the packing material within the box.

He pulled a bottle of wine and a sealed envelope out of the box. He handed the bottle of wine over to Gabe, and looked at the envelope. "Gabriel and Kevin" was written on the front in Rudy's clear even script. Kevin hated that it bothered him that Rudy had listed Gabe's name first.

Gabe turned the wine bottle in his hands, carefully studying the label.

"It's a wine from an Ohio winery," he said.

"Wow," Kevin said. "I would imagine you wouldn't come

across too many Ohio wines in Spain."

Gabe nodded absently as he looked at the wine bottle. There was an illustration of a wood carving of a large black raven, and underneath it was printed "Raven's Nest." Below that was written "a wine from the islands of Lake Erie." At the very bottom of the label were the words "Don't give up the split!"

It was a Riesling, Rudy's favorite wine. Gabe had always found Rieslings too sweet, and had always teased him about his sweet tooth for the dessert wine.

"Why would he have us travel all this way for a bottle of wine?" Kevin asked.

"I have no idea. Open the envelope, and let's see if he bothered to explain."

Kevin tore the end off the envelope and pulled out a single piece of paper. He blew into the end of the envelope and peered inside to make sure there were no other contents not immediately apparent.

"It looks like another letter."

Gabe pulled his chair around next to Kevin so that they could read the letter at the same time. It was dated almost three years earlier.

Dearest Kevin and Gabriel—
I am so pleased that you have come so far. When I was

creating the messages that brought you here, I was concerned it was too convoluted. I should have known it would prove to be no problem for my smart boys!

You have undoubtedly met the lovely Mora Garza. I have known her for nearly sixty years, and I would trust her with my life. (And, in some ways, I guess that I have.) Every gay man has one woman in his life who, if not for a certain twist of DNA, he would have married. Mora Garza is that woman for me.

I thank you for entertaining me and this quest so far. I know it has been a lot to ask, but I can only ask you to believe me—it is of the utmost importance.

I have always been most fortunate in my life, and I fully believe that my encounter with the Tzohar that cold Winter night so many years ago set the positive path of my life. I have always believed that for those to whom much has been given, much is expected. That is why I have always tried to give of myself—both of my money and my knowledge. Give a man a fish and he eats for a day; teach a man to fish and he eats for a lifetime. It is for that reason that I have always striven to honor the fishermen.

My best—

R.

Kevin picked up the letter and flipped it over to the back side then back again He picked up the now empty envelope and shook it over the table.

"What the hell?" he said in a frustrated tone. "That's it?"

"I'm afraid it looks that way. Just the letter and the bottle of wine."

"But it doesn't make any sense! The letter was rambling, and the wine makes no sense at all. For Christ's sake—we've come all the way to fucking Spain!" Kevin pounded his fist down on the table.

"I don't know what to say. It makes no sense to me either."

"I can't believe we've come this far for nothing," Kevin said sighing.

Both turned when Mora Garza came out of the kitchen, holding a large pitcher.

"It sounds as though you boys may not have been happy with what Rudolph left for you," she said, walking toward them.

"Yes, ma'am," Gabe said. "I guess you could say that."

"Well," she said. "I have something that will take the edge off. It's my famous homemade sangria."

Kevin gave her a wide smile. "Señora Garza, I can't imagine anything sounding better right now."

She poured them each a glass of Sangria, and both drank quickly.

"This is the best sangria I've ever tasted, Senora Garza,"

Gabe said.

"Please, call me Mora."

"Of course—Mora."

"I took the liberty of renting a few rooms for you in the hotel next door," she said. "I imagine you will be staying in Estepona for a few days?"

"We're not exactly sure," Gabe said. "We're afraid that we may be on somewhat of a wild goose chase."

Mora Garza laughed loudly. "Oh yes, I know that Rudolph can make you feel that way. But, I have complete faith that he knew exactly what he was doing—and he brought you here for a reason."

Gabe and Kevin looked at each other across the table. Neither one could completely share Mora's confidence.

Mora Garza raised her glass. "To Rudolph!" she said.

"To Rudolph," both Kevin and Gabe said simultaneously, raising their glasses to Mora's.

For the next few hours they told mutual stories of their time with Rudolph Zeffner, laughing and enjoying the memories of a man who had meant so much to all of them. It was at about the third pitcher of sangria when Gabe realized that he was getting very drunk. He looked over at Kevin, who was laughing hysterically at a story Mora was telling about Rudolph and a practical joke played on a Swiss tourist. He was sure Kevin was pretty intoxicated as well.

They continued to sit there, laughing and talking until the late hours of the night. Parties came and went at *Beber Gayo*, many of them commenting at what a wonderful time Mora Garza seemed to be having with the visiting Americans. Gabe had long lost track of how many pitchers of sangria they had consumed, and he was a little bit embarrassed that a woman in her eighties seemed to be holding her liquor much better than he was.

Shortly after Midnight, Mora Garza announced that it was time for her to say good night. Gabe and Kevin rose and warmly hugged her. Both could see why Rudy felt the way he did about her.

They practically stumbled out of *Beber Gayo* and into the street.

"Do you think that's our hotel there?" Kevin asked, heavily slurring his words.

"There's only way to find out," Gabe said, laughing at a joke only he seemed to get.

They walked across the street, and into the lobby of the small hotel. Gabe attempted to keep his composure as much as possible as he spoke with the desk clerk. He paid for his and Kevin's rooms in cash, but was having a difficult time counting out the exact amount. The desk clerk smiled patiently at him; he was used to dealing with drunk tourists. Being next door to *Beber Gayo*, he was well aware of the reputation of Señora Garza's famous sangria.

Gabe got the keys to Kevin's and his rooms, and they stumbled toward the elevators. Luckily the lobby was empty except for the sparse hotel staff, so their embarrassment over their current condition was limited.

"What room am I in?" Kevin asked, much more loudly than he had intended.

"Shhhh!," Gabe said, nearly as loudly and putting his index finger in front of his mouth in an exaggerated stage gesture. "You're in room 405 and I'm in 507."

They took the elevator to the fourth floor, and headed down the hallway toward Kevin's room.

"I'll see you in the morning," Gabe said handing Kevin his room key. "Then we'll try to figure out what in the hell that old man was trying to tell us."

Kevin took the key card and directed it toward the slot about the door handle, badly missing. He tried again and dropped the card.

"Jesus," Gabe said laughing. "You are so damn drunk."

He picked the key up off the floor and tried a third attempt at opening the door. He missed the card slot as well.

"You're as drunk as I am," Kevin said laughing.

On the fourth attempt, the card fit into the slot and the door opened suddenly. Gabe and Kevin both stumbled into the room, and fell against the inside wall. Both were laughing as Gabe stopped Kevin from falling and pulled him up to eye level.

Later, neither one could be sure who initiated the kiss, but once it started it did not really matter. Kevin kicked the door closed, as he and Gabe continued kissing; stumbling toward the bed.

Gabe never made it to room 507 that night.

Chapter Thirty

Gabe awoke to brilliant sunlight shining through the hotel room window. The window was open slightly, and the rich smell of salt air wafted into the room. He took a deep breath and slowly opened his eyes. His head throbbed, and his mouth was cotton dry. For a moment, he did not remember where he was.

He sat up and turned to look at Kevin who was laying asleep beside him. All of a sudden, the reality of the situation came flooding back to him.

Oh, my God, he thought. *What the hell was I thinking?*

He crawled out from under the covers, and got out of bed as gently as possible so he would not wake Kevin. While he knew he would have to face Kevin—and this situation—sooner or later, his head hurt too badly right now to contemplate it.

He looked around the floor for his clothes. Finding only his tee shirt and jeans, he decided to make do with that. Luckily, it still felt like Summer in Estepona and he could get by with being lightly dressed. He picked up his cell phone and wallet from the desk and slipped them into his pocket. He tripped over his own shoes on the way to the door.

Out on the street he turned toward the marina and started walking. He had no idea where he was going, or what exactly he was going to do once he got there. He just knew that facing Kevin right now was impossible; he needed some time to think. He wished he would have found his sunglasses on his slinking escape from the room—the glare was intensifying his headache.

He turned to walk along the Avenue de Juan Carlos which ran perpendicular to the waterfront, and headed into the village center. What was in that sangria, anyway? That was supposed to be a light weight drink…although, he supposed after five or six consecutive pitchers there was really no such thing.

How could he have slept with Kevin? If someone would have told him a week ago that he would have been speaking to Kevin—let alone sleep with him—he would have told them they were crazy. (Actually, he probably would not have been so polite.) But, a lot of things had changed in a week. Rudy was dead and now he and his ex-boyfriend were half-way around the world on this crazy quest.

He felt guilty, even though he was not sure why—Kevin was certainly no innocent bystander in this himself. He wondered if Kevin would be having the same internal dialogue with himself as he was having now.

He wondered if deep down he somehow really wanted this to happen. After all, it was not like he stopped loving Kevin the day Kevin told him he was leaving him for Rudy.

Granted, his feelings toward him turned quite a bit darker—much more akin to hate. But still, it did not change the depth of his feelings. He had read enough literary criticism to know that the opposite of love was not hate—it was indifference. And, indifferent would never describe his feelings for Kevin.

Estepona's town center was starting to come to life as the shopkeepers began business for the day. He smiled at several people as he walked by. He was sure he must look really bad. If he looked half as bad as he felt right now he would be quite the sight.

He was just thinking about heading back to the hotel to face Kevin when he nearly ran right into the memorial in the center of town. It was comprised of a large circular fountain with large stone wall rising vertically from its center. The stone wall was about ten feet tall and five feet wide and contained various engravings. At the top of the wall were the words *Dedicated to the Brave Fishermen of Estepona* in Spanish. He recalled the closing line from Rudy's most recent letter.

It is for that reason that I have always striven to honor the fishermen.

He looked closely at the engravings on the stone wall. There were a series of panels depicting various scenes. Most of the scenes had to do with fishing or sea scenes. However, it was the panel in the bottom left corner of the wall that captured Gabe's attention.

In that panel there was a depiction of a raven with what appeared to be a glowing orb behind it. Below that was an engraving that appeared to be an arrowhead. Below that was written:

KLESH TSIN-TLITI A-CHI D-AH CHA KLESH A-KHA TSAH

More Navajo? Gabe pulled his cell phone out of his pocket and began to take pictures of the fisherman memorial, carefully zooming in on the mysterious panel. He walked around the memorial to see if there was anything else which looked unusual. He noticed a small bronze plaque on the edge of the fountain.

Made possible by the financial generosity of Senor Rudolph Zeffner

Gabe continued to take several pictures with his cell phone, then e-mailed them to his mail account. He would want to look at the details on a larger screen as soon as he got back to the hotel.

He was surprised at the rush of adrenalin he got with the find of this information. For a moment he forgot all about the uncomfortable situation with Kevin; right now, all he was thinking about was getting back to the hotel and telling him of his discovery.

✳ ✳ ✳ ✳

Over four thousand miles away in a cheap motel room in Columbus, Ohio, Noah Dew was alerted to an incoming e-mail message from the tone emitting from Gabriel Patrick's stolen laptop.

He walked over to the laptop and clicked on the message so that he could view the full text. It had been sent by Patrick himself from his cellular phone to his regular e-mail account. The only contents of the message were a series of photographs which appeared to be of a fountain and some sort of engravings.

Most of the engravings seemed to have something to do with fishing scenes, but the one photographed with the most detail was one of a bird with a glowing circle behind it. Noah Dew recognized it immediately from years of hearing the stories passed down from his grandfather and father—it was the Gem of Holy Light.

He looked at the words written below it. Was that German? Was it Spanish? Having spent nearly his entire life sequestered within the confines of the religious society had left him with little practical knowledge of other cultures, languages, or people. But, that doesn't matter he thought. He did know how to use the Internet, and from there all the shortcomings in his personal knowledge could be redeemed.

He jotted down the words in the photo and started the Internet search engine.

Chapter Thirty One

CINCINNATI, OH

Namir Yosef stood at the two-way mirror in the observation room overlooking two interrogation rooms at the FBI field office in Cincinnati. He had arrived in the southwestern Ohio city a few hours before, and had come immediately to the field office.

He had been dispatched here by his Mossad superiors who had been alerted by the FBI. The men in custody were on a watch list authored by the Mossad and distributed among various collegial agencies, including the FBI, CIA, and MI5. It was one of the rare cooperative actives between international security agencies which began shortly after 9/11. After the subsequent bombings in Madrid and London, cooperation among the agencies became even stronger.

Ibriham and Asad Warsame had made their way onto the Mossad's watch list over two years ago. The two Somali nationals were known by the Israeli's to be part of a cell that has fervently sought the Tzohar for years. The brothers were assumed by the Mossad to have murdered an American tourist who was killed in England in 2005. The American had been the leader of a fundamentalist Christian church who had also made its sole mission to obtain the Tzohar. The Mossad agent also suspected the two men in the murder of

Rudolph Zeffner in Dallas a few days ago. Yosef wondered how many people had died over the millennia in the name of the Tzohar.

The Warsame brothers were arrested in Columbus the day before for a routine traffic violation. With the second largest Somali population in the United States, the Columbus police were well accustomed to arresting young Somali men for a variety of nuisance crimes. However, they were surprised to find that these two men were on a watch list by the FBI. The Columbus police contacted the FBI who had the men transferred to the nearest field office.

After determining that the Warsame's were on a reciprocal watch list by the Israelis, the FBI contacted the Mossad. The Mossad leadership then dispatched the Special Considerations task team, and less than twenty four hours later, Namir Yosef was half a world away in Ohio.

The door to the observation room opened behind him, and Namir turned to face the new arrival to the room.

"Hello," a tall blonde man said extending his hand, "I'm Mark Adman. I'm the Special Agent assigned to this case."

Namir returned the man's handshake. "I'm Namir Yosef of the Mossad. I'm the agent assigned to the case by the Israeli government."

"Well, welcome to Cincinnati Mr. Yosef. I'm just hoping that you didn't make this long trip for nothing."

"And, I as well Agent Adman."

Namir looked at the young FBI agent. He was tall and athletic looking; and looked to be no older than thirty at the most. From his relative youth, Namir assumed that this must be one of his first assignments with the bureau. It would appear that the FBI did not consider that the Warsame brothers posed a serious threat to American security.

"According to procedure, the bureau will conduct the interview, but you're welcome to observe," Agent Adman said. "From this observation area you'll be able to monitor both interview rooms. Two female agents will be conducting the interviews—we've found talking to a pretty girl tends to throw the Muslims off a bit."

Namir nodded in understanding. He was sure that these young Muslim men would find being interrogated by a young, pretty American female to be particularly distasteful. Maybe their discomfort would result in them saying more than they intended.

"Have you been able to track their recent movements?"

"Yes, pretty much," the agent said, studying the contents of a file folder. "They arrived in the U.S. on a Student Visa about two weeks ago and first landed in Minneapolis, which isn't too unusual. The Somali population in Minneapolis is even bigger than the one in Columbus. However, they never showed up for the start of classes at the University of

Minnesota."

"How long had they been in Columbus?"

"They say they headed to Columbus within a few days of arriving in the country; claimed they had family there and decided to try Ohio State instead of Minnesota. Just Big Ten rivalry, I'd guess," Agent Adman said, smiling at his own joke.

Namir ignored the young FBI agent's attempt at humor. "Do you believe that account to be true."

"Yes," he said, assuming his joke was just lost on the Israeli. "That story fits with the financial tracking we've done on them."

"Any evidence they may have visited Texas—Dallas specifically—over the past week?"

"Dallas? No, we can pretty much account for their movements from Minneapolis to Columbus, right up until they got pulled over for making that illegal U-turn on Cleveland Avenue yesterday."

Namir Yosef nodded his head in understanding. While the Warsame brother's apparent absence in Dallas did not mean one of their fellow cell members had not killed Zeffner, it certainly made the Mossad's theories about the murder more unlikely. Yosef turned to watch the two interviews being conducted.

The two female FBI agents who were interviewing the brothers separately were young and very attractive. Namir estimated that they were around Agent Adman's age—or even younger. Apparently, Cincinnati was a good training ground for new FBI agents.

While young, the women certainly knew what they were doing. They acted confident, authoritative, and slightly flirtatious all at the same time. The women seemed to make the Somali men very nervous. Namir imagined part of that stemmed simply from being in the custody of the FBI, but the female agents were certainly doing everything possible to heighten that discomfort.

He would give the Americans credit for one thing, over the past several years they had become very adept at pushing the right buttons when questioning extremist Muslims. Prior to September 11th, Namir believed that was a skill where only the Israelis could excel.

Regardless of the discomfort the Somalis were feeling, the interviews were pretty much fruitless. They both repeated the same story of arriving in Minneapolis, but being homesick for family and closer acquaintances, they quickly decided to head to Columbus instead.

The female agent questioning Ibriham Warsame asked him why he thought that the Israeli intelligence agency would have the Warsame brothers on a watch list.

"How should I know why the Jew infidels do anything?" he replied, sneering.

The interviews with both brothers continued similarly for the next half hour. The Warsame brothers stuck to their story, and swore that they knew of no reason why the Israelis would be watching them. Finally, Agent Adman spoke into the ear pieces that both female agents were wearing, and announced that it was time to halt the interviews.

"I'm sorry you came all this way for nothing," Agent Adman said addressing Namir. "But, there's not much more we can do here. A simple traffic violation doesn't warrant involvement by the bureau."

Namir sighed. "Yes, I understand. What will be done with the Warsame brothers now?"

"We'll turn them over to the INS. They violated the terms of their student visas, so they'll most likely be deported."

"Is there any chance I could have a few minutes to speak with them? With an agent present, of course."

Agent Mark Adman looked at him and carefully considered the request. It was not exactly kosher with protocol—the agent smiled, enjoying his private pun—but what harm could it do? They were always being instructed to do what was possible to improve their relationships with allied agencies, and this seemed a very easy way to work toward that goal.

"Ok," the agent said. "We can do that, but I'll need to be present during the questioning."

"Of course, of course. That's only proper since they are officially in the custody of the FBI."

Agent Adman had both Ibriham and Asad Warsame moved into the same interview room, and the agent and Namir entered a few minutes later. The Warsame brothers were sitting on the same side of a conference table, and Adman pulled out a chair facing them. Namir followed his lead.

"We just have a few more questions for you before the INS agents arrive to pick you up. This is Namir Yosef of the Mossad. That's an Israeli agency in case you didn't know."

He watched both brothers closely to see if the arrival of the Israeli agent changed the demeanor of the men. Both looked straight ahead, and showed no reaction to what the FBI agent had just said.

"Gentlemen," Namir Yosef said. "I appreciate the opportunity to speak with you."

Both Somali men continued to look straight ahead. They seemed to have regained some composure since their interviews with the female agents, and had apparently decided to completely ignore the men now questioning them.

"I take it you still have failed in your quest to find the Tzohar?"

The Somali men could no longer feign indifference. Their eyes grew wide as they stared at Namir. They were visibly shaken.

"*Kaah*," Asad Warsame whispered.

"Yes," Namir said. "*The light.* I know all about the light—probably much more than you two do."

"You fucking Jew," Ibriham Warsame snarled in broken English. "You infidels know nothing of the light."

"Well," Namir said, rising away from the table. "We infidels may know a little more than you think."

Mark Adman followed his lead and also rose from the table. He seemed somewhat surprised by the entire exchange between the Somalis and the Israeli agent.

Namir reached the door to the exit of the interview room, and turned back to the Warsame brothers. "Keep in mind," he said with a smirk. "A Jew has possessed the Tzohar for most of its history." He turned the door handle and walked out of the room. He heard one of the brothers slam his fist down on the table as he disappeared through the door.

In the hallway, Mark Adman looked at him quizzically. "So, what was that all about?"

"Just the superstitions of religious fanatics," Namir said. "But, they have no information that will be of use to our agency." He reached out and shook the FBI agent's hand. "But on behalf of my government, we thank you for your assistance."

Mark Adman nodded and returned the handshake. He

gave his business card to the Mossad agent, and a few minutes later escorted him out of the building.

Chapter Thirty Two

Gabe's trip back to the hotel was a cross between a brisk walk and a slow jog. He was anxious to get back and look up the new code in the Navajo dictionary, but most of all he was anxious to see Kevin. He could not wait to share this latest discovery with him.

He walked into the lobby of the hotel and was heading toward the small elevator when he spotted Kevin sitting at a table in the cafe off the lobby. A massive omelette and a pile of link sausages sat on the table in front of him.

"Hey," Kevin said as Gabe approached. "I woke up with a raging hangover and craving greasy food. Where did you disappear to?"

"I wanted to take a walk…"

"Gabe, I don't know why I…"

"Stop—there's no reason to get into this heavy conversation right now," he paused for a moment, and looked intently at Kevin, then whispered. "I'm pretty sure I've found the next clue."

"What?" Kevin asked, his demeanor immediately changing. "How? Where?"

"In town—there's a memorial art piece dedicated to the fisherman of Estepona. From the plaque, Rudy commissioned and funded it."

"*It is for that reason that I have always strove to honor the fishermen*," Kevin said, repeating the closing line from Rudy's most recent letter. "He keeps pointing us in the right direction—I guess we just have to keep our eyes open and look."

"There were some odd things on the memorial. I took some pictures to show you, but first I want to grab my laptop," He paused for a moment. "Umm…can I borrow your room key?" For a moment, the embarrassment from the night before returned.

Kevin handed him the room key card without comment. Gabe took it from him, and was back at the table within five minutes with his laptop. Gabe booted it up and was relieved to detect a wireless internet signal.

He opened up his e-mail and double-clicked on the messages containing the photos sent from his cell phone. He was so anxious to show Kevin the photos that he failed to notice that the messages were not marked as new mail; they had been previously opened.

The first photo opened on the full seventeen inch screen, and was a close up of the unusual carved panel above the fountain.

"The rest of the design was focused around fishing and sea scenes, but his panel really stood out."

"So, I'm guessing the glowing circle is meant to represent

the Tzohar?" Kevin asked.

"Yes, that was my theory."

"And, what's this? It looks like an Indian arrowhead."

"Yeah," Gabe said. "That was my guess too. The words below it look like more Navajo language."

"Well, at least he's consistent," Kevin said.

"I guess he figured if the Nazis never figured it out, it was safe to use again here."

Gabe brought up the online Navajo dictionary and carefully compared each word etched on the panel of the fishermen memorial.

"It says *Smithson*," he said, after a few minutes of close study.

"*Smithson*? You mean like *James Smithson*?" Kevin asked.

Gabe looked thoughtfully for a moment. "James Smithson—the founder of the Smithsonian Institute? Hmmm... that's an interesting thought. The Smithsonian recently opened a new museum dedicated to the history of Native Americans."

Kevin smiled widely. "It's actually called the Museum of the American Indian. And, something else pretty interesting—Rudy consulted on exhibit design."

"Really? What exhibit did he consult on?"

"I'm not sure exactly. I know it had something to do

with religious legends and iconography of the Indians. You know, his normal gig. So, are you thinking that maybe the Tzohar is hidden somewhere in the museum?"

"Possibly, or maybe it will only lead us to the next clue," Gabe said, sitting back in his chair and crossing his arms. "But, either way, I think that Washington, DC is our next destination."

❋ ❋ ❋ ❋

After typing in the strange words from the photos in Gabriel Patrick's intercepted e-mail, Noah Dew was faced with nearly three hundred returns from the search engine. Almost all of the suggested articles focused on the Navajo Indian language.

Navajo? Dew was perplexed at its meaning. The realization also infuriated him even more—how dare the old Nazi use the tongue of Godless savages to use in his theft and hiding of the Holy Light?

Dew clicked on the first suggested article and read it carefully. It explained how the Navajo language had been as a secret code by the Allies during World War Two—the only code never broken by the Germans. Suddenly, Zeffner's choice of Navajo made a little more sense—perhaps it was some attempt at revenge in the old Nazi's mind.

The second article included a complete Code Talkers dictionary. Each of the "words" contained in the photos from Spain seemed to represent a letter of the alphabet in English. Noah Dew checked each set of characters carefully.

They spelled out the word *smithson*. Noah Dew sighed loudly, closed his eyes and rubbed them hard with his balled fists. There were yet still more riddles from the old German sodomite. He found himself surprised at the depth of hatred he felt for the man who he had only met for a few moments.

Dew entered the search term *smithson* into the search engine. This time he was confronted with over two million results. He slammed his fist down hard on the cheap hotel desk, and heard the cracking of the pressboard of which it was made. Unlike his earlier search, there seemed to be cohesion tying these results together.

He glanced half-way down the first page of results and saw that there were several articles pertaining to the Smithsonian Institute. He clicked on the first of these articles, and read that the Smithsonian had been founded and financed by James Smithson, a wealthy British scientist who bequeathed in his will to the United States government the funds to create an "establishment for the increase and diffusion of knowledge among men." That establishment is what became the museums of the Smithsonian.

He read a little further, and learned that there were

seventeen separate museums that make up the Smithsonian Institute. Seventeen museums, covering hundreds of acres of exhibit space, and a collection of over one hundred and thirty six *million* items. How would he know where to even begin looking?

He went back to Gabriel Patrick's e-mail and pulled up the pictures from Spain again. In the same photo with the etching of the Holy Light and the Navajo words was something he had not noticed before—it looked like an Indian arrowhead.

He went back to the search engine and modified his keywords. He typed in *Smithsonian Indian* and *Zeffner*, then clicked the search button. Less than twenty articles were returned. All mentioned an exhibit developed at the Smithsonian Museum of the American Indian by the renowned art historian, Rudolph Zeffner.

As he sat staring at the computer and pondering the meaning, his thoughts were interrupted by the sound of another incoming e-mail. This time it was a flight purchase confirmation from the travel web service. Gabe Patrick had purchased two one-way tickets from Malaga, Spain to Washington, DC.

Noah Dew sat back and smiled. He was grateful for the stolen computer and how easy it was making it for him. He too would be heading to Washington, DC where he would be greeting his newly found friends again in person—and this time he intended for the next meeting to be their very last.

Chapter Thirty Three

Namir Yosef sat in the Delta Sky Club and sipped a cup of hot, black coffee. American coffee was not the same as the strong thick drinks he enjoyed at home, but it certainly served its purpose. He had come straight to the airport from his meeting at the Cincinnati FBI field office. He glanced at his watch—he had been on the ground in the United States for less than ten hours.

He had nothing really against the American Midwest, but still he could not wait to get out of here. He had never felt completely comfortable in the United States. His flight would leave Cincinnati in a little over an hour, then it was a short flight to JFK where he would board an El Al flight home to Israel. Once on El Al he would finally feel back in his own element.

He sat in an overstuffed leather chair near the large windows that overlooked one of the runways. From this vantage point he could see dozens of planes circling in the skies above the Cincinnati/Northern Kentucky International Airport waiting for their turns to come back to Earth. He still thought it somewhat odd that the busiest airport that served Ohio was not actually in Ohio at all—it was in Kentucky.

He looked around the private club's lounge, carefully observing the few people around him. It was surprisingly quiet in the Sky Club for rush hour during the peak of the business travel week. Maybe the economy was really as bad as all the gloom and doom sayers in the media would have everyone believe.

His attention turned to a young family sitting in a cluster of similar leather chairs to his right. The parents were well dressed and appeared to be in their mid to late thirties. Their child looked to be around ten, and she was complaining vehemently to her mother about something. The mother was unsuccessfully trying to reason with the girl, but her voice was growing more shrill by the moment. The husband sat staring at something on his Blackberry, and seemed to be completely oblivious to the ongoing angst between the females in his life occurring right in front of him.

He shook his head and returned his gaze out the window. *What my father would have done to me if I ever would have acted in such a way in public*, he thought.

His prejudice immediately chalked it up to bad American behavior. But, deep down, he knew that was not a fair observation. He could have witnessed the exact same scene playing out in Tel Aviv, or London, or Cairo, or Mumbai—impoliteness and rude behavior was the world's problem now. Still, it gave him some sort of comfort to blame it on this upper middle class American family sitting in front of him.

He felt his cell phone vibrate within the inside pocket of

his suit jacket. He looked at the display screen to see it was the incoming number of Anon Rozen. He had instructed his junior agent only to contact him if the Mossad had obtained any additional information about Patrick and Hurst, or if there was any new information on the location of the Tzohar.

"Yosef," he said simply to identify himself as he answered the phone.

"Sir, this is Agent Rozen. I'm sorry to bother you, but we have some additional information on Gabriel Patrick and Kevin Hurst. They've purchased two tickets from Spain to Washington, DC and their flight leaves within the hour."

"I see," Yosef said, his mind quickly churning on reasons why Washington might be the new destination for the men. "Do we have any information on where or why they might be heading there?"

"No sir, unfortunately we do not. However, the Christian extremist we've been surveilling is also on the move. We have reports that he left Columbus over an hour ago, heading East on Interstate 70. Sir, that route could also be taking him to Washington."

Namir Yosef said nothing for a few seconds as he processed this new information.

"Sir?" the voice of the junior officer on the other end of the line asked. "Have we lost the connection?"

"No, I'm still on the line. After the interrogation, it's

apparent that the Somali's were not directly involved with the Zeffner *situation*." He deliberately avoided using the word *murder*, assuming that if anything would distract the rude family from their own drama, that could be it.

"So," Yosef continued. "That would make Noah Dew and the members of the Millfield Valley Holiness Church our chief suspects."

"Yes, sir," the voice on the other side of the Transatlantic phone call said.

"Unfortunately, that makes our job somewhat more challenging. We'll have no choice now but to actively involve the Americans."

"Is that absolutely necessary, sir?"

"Yes, when it was Somali nationals it was one thing, but when our target is a group from the American Bible Belt, we have no choice but to involve them."

The younger agent said nothing, but he knew his superior was right.

"I'll follow up with our contacts in the FBI and bring them into the loop. I'll be changing my flight plans. It may finally be time to let Patrick and Hurst in on exactly what kind of mess they've gotten themselves into."

Yosef quickly and somewhat abruptly ended the call with his subordinate. Generally speaking, he was a man that had little patience for pleasantries. But that was especially true when it was his responsibility to protect one of the greatest treasures in the history of human kind.

Putting on his best show smile, he walked up to the ticket agent located within the airline club and proceeded to change his flight plans.

Chapter Thirty Four

Gabe sat back in the leather covered seat on the Airbus A340 and closed his eyes. This was his second transatlantic flight in as many days and his body was more than feeling the toll. Of course, the remnants of the hangover and last night's indiscretions were not doing him much good either. Thank God for first class—after this experience he may never be able to bring himself to fly coach again.

The plane was still sitting at the jet bridge as the remaining coach passengers filed onto the plane, heading to their tiny cramped seats. He looked at them with a mix of sympathy and gloating. He closed his eyes, and was starting to doze off when Kevin's voice startled him.

"So, about last night…"

"A movie from the 1980s, if I recall correctly. Rob Lowe's wang was in it."

Kevin chuckled. "Ok, point taken. There will be plenty of time for serious conversations later. Just remember—you were the one always accusing me of running away from the tough talks."

"Yeah, I know. Maybe I've decided there really were some merits to your approach," Gabe said, smiling warmly at Kevin.

"Although, we also haven't had a lot of time for small talk

either since this whole thing started."

"Small talk?" Like what?"

"Like, what's the deal with the antique shop in Olde Towne? Last thing I knew you were on track for tenure and full professorship. Rudy had mentioned that you left Ohio State, but I had assumed it was to move to another university."

"Well, I'm sure Rudy felt I was committing career suicide, so it doesn't surprise me that he wanted to spare you the details. The truth is that I was fired—I shot off my big mouth to the boss once too often."

Kevin nodded, and said nothing for a few seconds. "Well, you always did have a much lower tolerance than most for the political bullshit. Remember that big blow up with the visiting adjunct professor from USC?"

Gabe smiled. He recalled the many evenings he had spent complaining to Kevin about the various frustrations and petty arguments of his work life at the university. Kevin had never commented much, and Gabe assumed that he was never really listening. Apparently he had been wrong.

"So, you decided to open an antique shop? I didn't think most gay men did that until they hit sixty or so?" Kevin shot Gabe a mischievous grin.

"It's more than an antique shop. Yeah, it started out that way…antique shop and gallery. But, it's turned into a lot more. I really feel like I'm helping people now."

"Helping people? Through antique shopping?"

"People come to me to help them find important things they've lost throughout their lives. Granted it's things like glassware and jewelry, but it represents a lot more to them— it's part of their lives. I help people reunite with some of their greatest treasures, and it feels really good."

"You're doing the same thing now for Rudy."

"Yeah," Gabe said. "I hadn't thought of it that way, but I guess you're right."

"So, what's the business called? I didn't see any signs at your door."

"It doesn't really have a name. At first I just called it the 'Patrick Gallery' but that doesn't seem adequate anymore. But, I just can't think of anything better."

"Well, I'll think about it and help you come up with something. It sounds like a great business, and it deserves a worthy name. I'm happy that you're happy."

Gabe looked at Kevin and smiled. He knew deep down that he sincerely meant what he had just said. In that moment, he knew why he had always felt the way he had about Kevin. The old adage *time heals all wounds* never felt truer.

He spoke to break the awkward silence. "So, what about you?"

"What about me?" Kevin asked.

"What's going on with your career now? You had mentioned that you and Rudy were arguing over a tour offer you had received?"

"Yeah, it was with a show I had been doing in Dallas that was going on tour. It was a musical based on the life of a young gay man living in 1950s Cuba. I wrote most of the music for it."

"Wow," Gabe said, genuinely impressed. "You scored an entire show?"

"Well, I scored most of an entire show. Like everything else, it was a collaboration."

"Still, that's absolutely amazing that you were part of creating something like that. And, now your show is going to tour?"

"Yeah, we started off in a small theater in Oak Lawn, then started playing a bigger venue in Dallas. The guy who produced it for our group lined up some financial backers and got the money together for a ten city tour. If it works out, they're thinking we could take it to Broadway or London—or maybe at least Toronto."

"Kevin, that's fantastic! That's pretty much your dream come true. And you weren't going to go? No wonder Rudy was so pissed off at you."

"Yeah, I know," Kevin said. "The timing just didn't feel right. I didn't feel comfortable leaving Rudy alone. You haven't seen much of him in the last several years, but he was aging quickly. I worried about him."

"And, now?"

"And, now what?"

"Not to be hard-hearted, but Rudy's gone. There's nothing holding you back now—and you know this is what he'd want you to do."

"Things have been so crazy since Rudy was killed I haven't had a chance to think about it."

"You should think about it. There's nothing standing in your way now."

"Yeah, I guess," Kevin said hesitantly.

Gabe looked at him quizzically, silently gesturing for him to continue.

Kevin continued to speak. "I'm afraid of what will happen if everything I've always wanted does come true, you know? What if it's not like I thought it would be, or what if I fail? Then what?"

"What if you don't try and always wished you had? Kevin, take it from a man who has been there. There is no worse way to go through life than always wondering *what if*."

Kevin looked at Gabe and smiled. He leaned into Gabe's seat and kissed him on the cheek.

"Thanks, Gabe," he said smiling. "You know, Oprah's got nothing on you."

Gabe laughed. Grateful for the levity breaking the serious conversation.

The Iberian airlines flight was fourth in line for take off as it slowly taxied. A few minutes later it sped down the runway and raised in the western evening sky. As the plane began heading toward the United States, both Gabe and Kevin drifted off to sleep.

Chapter Thirty Five

Molly Newman was scared.

Normally, such a base emotion would not apply to her—it simply was not her style. However, this time felt different. She knew her friend Gabe was in serious trouble, but she did not really understand how or why. Even worse, she had absolutely no idea how to help him.

Typically, not much scared Molly. In addition to the nearly fifteen years she had spent on the police force in one of the most crime riddled areas of the fifteenth largest city in the country, she had also seen front line combat. She had gone into the Marines right after high school as a way to pay for college and she had seen front line service in the first Gulf War. Most people tended to think of Gulf War One as not being as bloody or traumatic as some other combat operations in American history. However, she could tell a few stories that would quickly—and graphically—change anyone's mind about that.

Molly had been raised a military brat, as her father had spent his career in the Marines. She had moved from town to town and school to school as a child, so she never really put down permanent roots or made lifelong friends. The lifestyle had the advantage of making her tough and confident. She never feared new situations, and always felt perfectly comfortable being dropped into any kind of scenario.

When she was a child her father had been doing his third tour of Vietnam when he was declared missing in action and assumed dead. For nearly a month, Molly, her mother, and her baby brother lived with the knowledge that they probably would never see her father again. Molly was deeply affected by the quiet strength her mother had shown. She simply picked up and started doing the things she new she needed to do to take care of her family—closely following the "what if" plans she and Molly's father had made over their years together.

It turned out that Molly's father had not been killed, but rather injured and misidentified in a field hospital. The family was finally alerted that he was alive, and after several more weeks of recuperation he was able to return home.

It was the happiest day of Molly's young life when she saw her father get off that plane, nearly six weeks after she had accepted the fact that he was dead. She had also never seen her mother as glowing or as joyous as she had been that day.

But, Molly never forgot how her mother was prepared to pick up the pieces and move on when she believed that to be her fate. She did not wallow in self-pity; she did not curse God for her bad luck—she simply did what she needed to do. Molly decided she would always show the same kind of strength and courage that her mother had shown.

That strength always came easily when it just involved Molly's life and well being, but now that it involved her close friend, she felt completely and utterly helpless. Normally, Molly did not develop close relationships. Other than her partner Vickie whom she had been with since they were freshmen at Bowling Green State University, she never really found herself able to get too close to others.

But, her friendship with Gabe had been different. She had first met Gabe when she had been assigned as the police force liaison to the Olde Towne East community association. He was new to the group and the neighborhood, and was anxious to get involved.

They hit it off from the start. They had similar senses of humor, and a similar distaste for the pretentious attitudes that some of the association members would exhibit. They spent a lot of time chuckling over the sometimes outrageous behavior of the others. Especially the group's president— *nothing more pompous than some bitchy queen with a title*, Gabe would always say.

Molly had not only been immediately drawn to Gabe, but Vickie had been as well. Vickie was a history teacher in the Columbus City Schools, and she had always enjoyed talking with Gabe about art and religious history—even having Gabe come in and talk to several of her classes. Gabe's appear-ances in her classes were about as close as a lot of those kids would ever come to a college lecture hall, or even a museum for that matter.

Vickie had often said that if she and Molly were ever to have a baby, she wanted Gabe to be the donor. Molly would laugh it off, but deep down she knew that Vickie was serious. What's more, Molly knew she could get serious about the idea too. She always thought that she would try floating that idea with Gabe sometime—first as a joke to see how he would react. She realized that there was a ticking clock facing her though, and she could only afford to play coy for so long now.

But now, all that felt very far away. She had picked up on bits and pieces of communication that was occurring among her superiors, and she knew something was up. From what she could tell, neither Gabe or Kevin were still considered suspects in the murder of Rudolph Zeffner in Dallas, but there were agencies wanting to find them none-the-less. She wanted to come right out and ask what was going on—this was her friend they were talking about. But, she knew protocol prevented it.

Her phone buzzed and she jumped. It certainly was not like her to be so easily spooked by a sudden noise. It was her sergeant asking to speak with her right away. The chief of police and a few other "ranking officers" wanted to speak with her regarding an important case.

She quickly hung up the phone, rose from her desk,

and walked directly to the sergeant's office. She knocked quickly on the door, and was directed by a voice to come in. She walked into the office, and was confronted by the site of her immediate superior, the chief of police (who she had only met once before), and a third man whom she did not recognize.

The strange man rose and extended his hand to Molly.

"Officer Newman, I'm Special Agent Mark Adman of the FBI. We're anxious for your input on a case."

Molly sat down, and the sergeant's office door was closed behind her.

Chapter Thirty Six

The plane touched down in Washington, DC at nearly 4:00 P.M. Eastern Time. They had changed planes in Madrid and London, where they had abandoned the Iberian fleet and boarded the American Airlines plane that brought them to Washington.

As the plane wheels hit the hard pavement of the runway, Gabe startled from his dozing. He rubbed his eyes and looked at his watch. Although, it did him little good—over the past few days he had been in more time zones than he could count, and had no idea in which one his watch was currently inhabiting.

He fought the urge to turn on his cell phone to check out the local time. He had been purposely leaving it powered off to avoid being tracked. He knew Molly was a good friend, but she was also a cop. If there was an arrest warrant out for Kevin—and probably himself by this point for aiding and abetting a murder suspect—he had to make sure they had the information they needed before talking to the police.

"Ladies and Gentleman," the flight attendant's voice intoned over the plane's speakers. "Welcome to Washington, DC where the local time is 3:50 P.M." He continued on with some spiel about appreciating their business, but by that point Gabe had stopped listening. He now knew the time which was the immediate information he required.

Kevin stretched in the seat beside him, his arms reaching above his head. He cracked his knuckles, and yawned loudly.

"That must have been the fastest Transatlantic flight I've ever been on," Kevin said.

"Yeah, that's what happens when you sleep all the way from London," Gabe replied. "It's nearly four o'clock—the Smithsonian museums close at five-thiry."

Kevin nodded at Gabe's statement but said nothing. They really needed to get to the Museum of the American Indian this afternoon. They had to finish following the path Rudy had laid out for them, and end this crazy situation once and for all. He was on the lam from the law, and he did not like the feeling. They needed to get this whole thing resolved, and if that involved following Rudy's crazy clues to find some mystical Biblical treasure, so be it. But—he wanted to get it done quickly.

Kevin pulled out a Washington tour book from his knapsack that he had purchased from a bookstore in Heathrow Airport. He flipped to a set of color maps at the end of the book, and ripped out the pages.

"I don't think we'll need the restaurant and hotel reviews," he said, as Gabe looked at him quizzically. "The maps are all we're going to need."

He studied the map of the DC Metro closely.

"We can pick up the yellow line directly at the airport, pick up the Orange or Blue line at L'Enfant Plaza then take it straight to the Smithsonian Station. That would be faster than taking a cab considering traffic at this time of day."

Gabe nodded in agreement. He had questioned why Kevin had bought the guidebook in London, but considering neither of them felt comfortable using their cell phones and the convenient maps they provided, he was certainly glad now that he had. By necessity they were now "off the grid." They were going to have to do this one the old fashioned way.

They had no checked baggage, so they could de-plane quickly and head towards Immigration. They had no problems with customs in Madrid, but that was in a foreign country—he doubted that an unsolved murder in Dallas had somehow made it onto Interpol's radar. But now they were back in the United States, and he had no idea what sort of warrants might have gone out for them since the last time he spoke with Molly.

As they stood in line to approach the agent, Gabe tried not to look nervous or suspicious—a goal which was becoming more and more difficult by the second. He glanced at Kevin, and he returned a slight but pleasant smile. He knew Kevin was just as nervous as he was, but yet he appeared perfectly calm. The advantages of spending so much time in the theater, he imagined.

As his turn came, Gabe approached the Agent and offered a friendly smile. The agent looked at him, but no smile was returned.

"Travel is great, but it's always good to get back home," Gabe said, trying his hardest not to sound too nervous.

"Passport and forms please," the agent said, holding out his hand.

Gabe handed him his passport and immigration form he had completed twenty minutes earlier on the plane. He was consciously aware of his hand shaking, and he hoped that it was not as apparent to the agent as it was to him.

"To Spain and back in less than forty-eight hours," the agent said, looking up and meeting Gabe's gaze. "That's a pretty quick trip for a European vacation."

"Well, it wasn't really a vacation," Gabe said, attempting to keep his voice and manner light. "I own a small gallery and I was in Spain checking on a potential art acquisition for one of my clients. Unfortunately, it didn't work out."

Gabe searched the agent's face for any sign of disbelief, but the man's stoic expression did not change. He was pleased with himself and how easily he had told the story he and Kevin had concocted on the plane.

"Thank you, sir," the agent said, handing Gabe back his travel documents.

Kevin walked up to the agent and handed him his passport and immigration form. "Hey," he said as a casual greeting. From the way the agent looked at Kevin, Gabe feared it may have been a little too casual for this particular Civil Servant.

The agent looked at Kevin and studied his papers. "I assume you two are traveling together?"

"Yeah, we work together," Kevin said with a smile.

The agent nodded and handed Kevin's passport back to him.

"Please move forward, sir," the agent said, motioning for Kevin to depart the station.

Gabe breathed a sigh of relief as he and Kevin walked out of Immigration and into the busy airport terminal.

"See," Kevin said jovially. "I told you it would be a piece of cake. All it takes is a little acting."

Gabe rolled his eyes, and waited for his heart to stop its nervous pounding.

* * * *

Namir Yosef felt his cell phone vibrate in the inside pocket of his sport jacket. He pulled it out and looked at the incoming call identification on the Motorola's screen. It was Anon Rozen.

"Yosef," he said answering the phone.

"Sir, we have confirmation that Patrick and Hurst have landed at Reagan National in Washington," Anon Rozen said. "Would you like local agents dispatched to intercept? The FBI has been briefed and is collaborating."

"That will not be necessary," Yosef said. "I can tend to that task personally. Please inform our contact with the FBI that I'll contact him with additional information within the hour."

He terminated the call without waiting for a reply from his subordinate.

Anon Yosef's flight from Cincinnati to Washington had arrived several hours before Gabe and Kevin's flight from Spain, and he had been waiting for their arrival in the main terminal just outside of Customs.

As the two Americans walked through the terminal, Yosef followed them, keeping a discrete, yet constant distance between them. Tracking these civilians would be so easy that a first year cadet could do it.

Gabe and Kevin took the escalator down from the main terminal, following the signs toward the airport Metro Station.

Anon Yosef continued to follow.

Chapter Thirty Seven

The Orange Line train pulled into the Smithsonian Station at nearly 4:30 P.M. That only gave Gabe and Kevin an hour to get to the Museum of the American Indian and find the clue they were seeking. Of course, they had no idea what that clue would look like.

"Any idea where to go once we get to the museum?" Gabe asked Kevin.

Kevin closely studied a diagram of a map of the museum he had torn from the discarded guidebook.

"The project Rudy worked on was related to religious art of the Native Americans. I don't see it on this map, but there is a special exhibits area on the third floor. I guess we could start there."

They rose on the escalator out of the dim light of the Metro station and into the bright afternoon Autumn sky. Gabe squinted as his eyes became used to the sunlight. They walked across Jefferson Avenue and headed to the many sidewalks that crisscrossed the National Mall. From there they headed East toward the Capital Building.

The Museum of the American Indian was the latest addition to the Smithsonian family, and the newest building to be built on the National Mall. The five story building was one of the most striking works of architecture in the Capital historic area. Whereas most of the other buildings in the area were based on Greek or Roman classicism, this museum was built to resemble natural stone formations that have evolved over time, and invoked feelings of the Southwestern United States. Its orange-hued walls stood out from the stark white buildings which surrounded it.

"Rudy had said that it was a really beautiful building," Kevin said.

"Yeah, he was certainly right about that," Gabe replied. "I understand that pretty much all of the planning and design was done by Native American firms."

"A fancy museum doesn't seem like much restitution for the government pretty much wiping out your entire civilization, but whatever."

Gabe and Kevin turned right off the Mall and headed toward Third Street where the main doors of the museum faced. Before turning away, Gabe paused for a moment and looked at the Capital Building. No matter how many times he saw it, he was always amazed by the actual size of the building. Like the Grand Canyon or the Eiffel Tower, it was one of those things whose immensity could only be fully appreciated in person.

They walked through the front doors of the museum, and were greeted by the large open expanse of the four story atrium. Like the exterior, the interior of the Museum of the

American Indian was built to resemble a natural rock formation. The form of the atrium was like a large misshapen oval, whose walls curved around the structure.

Kevin walked over to a directory map of the museum near the entrance. "Yeah, this must be it," he said. "The 'Religious Iconography of Native America' display. It's in the special exhibits area on the third floor."

Gabe's eyes spanned the expanse of the atrium. Each floor of exhibit space opened to the atrium below. There were a series of stairways that formed a semi-circle along the back wall that climbed to all four stories of exhibit space, overlooking a large circular stage in the center of the floor.

Gabe motioned to the base of the stairs on the opposite of the atrium. "That stairway looks like the quickest route," he said.

Kevin nodded in agreement and they headed across the crowded floor to the stairs. Gabe was amazed at the large number of groups of children here. It seemed like every school in five surrounding states must have a field trip group here today.

They climbed the stairs, wrapping from the first floor to the second, then circling around to the set which led to the third level. The third floor seemed nearly as crowded as the first, with several groups of middle school-aged children milling about.

Kevin pointed to a banner hanging above a large door-way about one hundred feet ahead of them that read *Religious Iconography of Native America.*

"It's right over there."

Gabe and Kevin maneuvered through the groups of children and entered the exhibit area. The light was considerably dimmer in this area than the main floors of the museum, and soft tribal music added to the ambience. The space felt rich with an aura of spirituality and mysticism, and seemed to have a quieting effect on the tourists walking through.

A large display at the beginning of the space explained that the exhibit explored the various religious beliefs and legends of various tribes across North America. The description stated that the exhibit consumed over twenty-five thousand square feet of museum floor space.

"It's a big exhibit. Did Rudy work on any specific displays, or did he just consult on the overall project?" Gabe asked.

"He didn't talk much about it. I know he made a few trips to DC, and had several conference calls. I kind of got the feeling from Rudy's perspective that it really wasn't a major project."

"Funny," Gabe said. "Because it was obviously major enough for him to lead us to here."

They continued walking into the exhibit space, their eyes

quickly scanning the various displays. Gabe looked down at his watch; it was a few minutes before five.

Gabe stopped suddenly, and Kevin nearly ran into his shoulder.

"What's wrong?" Kevin asked.

Gabe pointed at a display about thirty feet in front of them. "Does that image of a bird look familiar to you?"

Kevin looked at it closely. "Yeah, it does look familiar, but I'm not sure why. Do you recognize it?"

Gabe smiled broadly. "Yes, I do. It's the same image of a raven that was on the wine bottle label that Rudy left for us in Spain."

Chapter Thirty Eight

Noah Dew was not stupid.

At least, he knew that he was not stupid. He was able to figure out the next clue that the old Nazi had left on the path to finding the Holy Light. He had even managed to arrive in Washington, DC hours before the two sodomites.

The drive from Columbus to Washington took a little over five hours. After being frustrated with city driving in Dallas, he decided not to face urban driving in another city, and decided to park his car at the Metro station in Greenbelt, Maryland and take the train into the city. He did not relish the idea of driving himself within the congested Capital area.

He missed his small hometown in Tennessee. He missed his family and friends, but most of all he missed his church. But soon, this quest would be over and his personal sacrifices would all be worth it. Once the Millfield Valley Holiness Church possessed the Holy Light, all the prophecies would be fulfilled. His father will not have died in vain.

He too had taken the Orange/Blue line to the Smithsonian station, but his trip had begun on the Green Line in Greenbelt. When he arrived at the Museum of the American Indian he walked around the exhibits, and had made a half-hearted effort to locate the next clue on his own. However, he quickly realized that he had no idea for what he was searching. He had intercepted enough information to lead him to this place, but he did not believe he could make it to the next step on his own. As much as he hated to admit it, he needed the help of the sodomites to find the Holy Light.

He sat down on a park bench on Third Street facing the museum. He sat and waited, keeping his eyes on the front of the museum while his mind wandered in a series of internal prayers.

He had no idea how much time passed while he was sitting there, but the sun had gone from high in the sky to just peeking behind the Washington Monument. His deep meditation was broken, and he was startled to attention by the sight of the two men walking toward the museum.

As Gabe Patrick and Kevin Hurst walked into the main entrance, Noah Dew stood and followed them inside.

Chapter Thirty Nine

Gabe and Kevin walked up to the exhibit featuring the raven that was clearly visible from across the room. It consisted of a series of displays in a glass case measuring about fifteen feet long and over ten feet tall. The large image of the raven reigned over the entire exhibit.

The central piece featured a Haida tribe legend titled *The Origin of Light*. It contained a series of smaller illustrations depicting the same raven, an Indian chief, and a young Native American girl. The first line of the story was larger than the rest, and began with the phrase *In the beginning the world was in total darkness*.

"Sounds a little familiar, doesn't it?" Gabe asked.

"Yeah, sounds like a total rip-off of the first line of the Bible," Kevin said, smiling.

"Except," Gabe replied. "It's older and came from thousands of miles away from where the Bible was written. Fascinating that they could still be so similar, huh?"

For the next several minutes, Gabe and Kevin read the rest of the legend in silence.

In the beginning the world was in total darkness.

The Raven, who had existed from the beginning of time, was tired of groping about and bumping into things in the dark.

Eventually the Raven came upon the home of an old chief who lived alone with his daughter. Through his slyness, the Raven learned that the old man had a great treasure. This was all the light in the universe, contained in a tiny box concealed within many boxes. At once the Raven vowed to steal the light.

He thought and thought, and finally came up with a plan. He waited until the old man's daughter came to the river to gather water. Then the Raven changed himself into a single hemlock needle and dropped himself into the river, just as the girl was dipping her water-basket into the river.

As she drank from the basket, she swallowed the needle. It slipped and slithered down into her warm belly, where the Raven transformed himself again, this time into a tiny human. After sleeping and growing there for a very long time, at last the Raven emerged into the world once more, this time as a human infant.

Even though he had a rather strange appearance, the Raven's grandfather loved him. But the old man threatened dire punishment if he ever touched the precious treasure box. Nonetheless the Raven child begged and begged to be allowed to hold the light just for a moment.

In time the old man yielded, and lifted from the box a warm and glowing sphere, which he threw to his grandson.

As the light was moving toward him, the human child transformed into a gigantic black shadowy bird-form, wings spread ready for flight, and beak open in anticipation. As the beautiful ball of light reached him, the Raven captured it in his beak!

Moving his powerful wings, he burst through the smoke-hole in the roof of the house, and escaped into the darkness with his stolen treasure.

And that is how light came into the universe.

"Wow. A warm and glowing sphere?" Kevin asked. "That sounds a lot like a certain something we're looking for, huh?"

"Yes, it certainly does. But, where is it? This display doesn't contain any feature that looks like it could be hiding the Tzohar."

Gabe and Kevin continued to read some of the smaller inscriptions that surrounded the main display. To the left of the raven story was a quote from a fifteenth century British philosopher:

In order for the light to shine so brightly, the darkness must be present.—Francis Bacon.

On the other side of the main display was an even older quote from a completely different part of the world:

We can easily forgive a child who is afraid of the dark; the real tragedy of life is when men are afraid of the light. —Plato

Finally, below the raven legend was a quote from one of

America's founding fathers:

Lighthouses are more helpful than churches. —*Benjamin Franklin*

"Seems like an odd hodgepodge of quotations, don't you think?" Kevin asked.

"Yes," Gabe said quietly. "Much too odd. It has to be telling us something."

"Look at how several characters in the quotes are emphasized."

Gabe looked closely at the quotes, then pulled out his cell phone and took several photos of the exhibit. He would have to risk having his cell phone powered on for a few seconds.

Kevin continued to study the quotes.

"Do the letters in bold spell anything? F-i-s-c-h-i-n-s-e-l?" he asked aloud.

Kevin's peripheral vision alerted him to something moving toward them quickly on his right. He turned toward the movement and stared.

"Oh, my God!" he said loudly.

Gabe turned as well, startled by the sound of fear in Kevin's voice.

"It's the man who attacked us at your house!"

Chapter Forty

The words barely had a chance to sink in, when Kevin began pushing Gabe in the opposite direction.

"We need to get the hell out of here," Kevin said, the panic clearly audible in his voice.

They pushed through a large group of touring Girl Scouts, and headed toward the exit at the far end of the exhibit space. The uniformed adult leaders looked at them with irritation as they pushed through the troops, and began a near run through the space.

Gabe turned to look over his shoulder and saw that the man had stopped and was staring at the raven exhibit. He turned and made direct eye contact with him. Gabe believed he had never seen hatred so pure in any other person's eyes in his entire life. The look was so disarming that he would have stopped dead in his tracks if Kevin had not pushed him forward. In his last glance at the man he saw that he too had begun moving again and was pursuing them.

They ran from the exhibit space through a very large crowd in the main hallway that was exiting from a theater for a film on contemporary Native American life that had recently ended. Normally, Gabe would find such a crowd annoying but now he found comfort in the safety of numbers. They continued to push through the crowd of a few hundred people. Gabe turned to look to see if the man was still chasing them, but all he could see was the crowd continuing to push out of the open theater doors.

They reached the stairs and began running down them taking two at a time, and trying to avoid knocking anyone down in front of them. They reached the second floor landing and were in a dead run to the next set of stairs, when Gabe heard someone calling him.

"Mr. Patrick, we need to talk," a man's voice said.

Gabe and Kevin stopped and turned toward the voice. A tall man with dark hair and a navy trench coat stepped from a small alcove near where the second floor exhibit space began.

"I know what's going on, and it's in your best interest to end this and come with me," the man said.

Gabe and Kevin froze, trying to comprehend what the man was saying to them. Who was he? Was he with the man who was chasing them? Gabe looked up to the stairs coming down from the third floor, and saw that the man with tattoos who had attacked Kevin in his house was coming toward them.

Both Gabe and Kevin looked back to the man who had called them. His trench coat parted slightly, and they could clearly see that he was carrying a gun in a holster.

"Shit!" Kevin exclaimed, and pushed Gabe forward toward the next set of stairs. They ran down the stairs, taking them two at a time. The groups of tourists ascending the stairs gave them dirty looks, but being impolite was the least of their worries right now.

They reached the main floor of the museum, and ran through the atrium. It was nearly five-thirty, and there was some sort of musical performance going on in the center of the floor, between them and the exit doors. Several men and women were playing a variety of Native American musical instruments in the daily closing ceremony. A huge crowd of people were surrounding the musicians, clapping and dancing.

Gabe looked back and saw that the man in the trench coat had now also reached the first floor and was pushing his way toward them. He looked up to the stairs coming down from the second floor and saw that the other man was coming as well.

They continued to push through the crowd, running directly between the musicians who looked at them with surprise. Most of the rest of the crowd just thought it was part of the show. They hit the front doors on a dead run and ran outside the museum. Daylight had faded quickly while they had been inside the museum, and the streets were packed with rush hour traffic.

Gabe turned and began heading back toward the Mall.

"Where are you going?" Kevin asked, grabbing his arm.

"Back to the metro station, we have to get out of here."

Kevin pulled him back in the opposite direction. "Federal Center is a lot closer, and we can transfer to other lines a few stops up. We need to get some distance between us and those guys—whoever they are."

Kevin began running down Third Street toward the Federal Center Metro Station, with Gabe closely following.

Chapter Forty One

N amir Yosef stood near the front doors of the Museum of the American Indian with three FBI agents who had been assigned to his task force by the bureau, and another Mossad agent who was stationed at the Israeli embassy in Washington.

"Sir," the other Mossad agent said to Yosef. "The targets have exited the museum. We feel they are most likely heading to one of the Metro trains."

"Unfortunately," one of the FBI agents said. "From this location you're only a few blocks from a half-dozen or so stations heading in all directions, so it makes determining their exact path somewhat difficult."

Yosef nodded in agreement. He understood that their resources were limited. His was a small task force that was operating below the radar of normal mainstream law enforcement.

He had worked through his recent contacts in the Cincinnati field office who had escalated his case up the chain of bureau command. Fortunately, the Mossad had a very strong working relationship with the counter terrorism units of the FBI. He had made his formal request for assistance directly to Washington through the Mossad headquarters in Tel Aviv.

The Mossad's official request was for assistance in apprehending multiple potential terrorists who were believed to be in the United States, and were pursuing a religious artifact belonging to Israel. (Yosef did not believe that was misleading at all, considering the important role that the Tzohar had played throughout the history of Judaism, he truly believed that the relic was the ancestral property of the Jewish State.)

The Americans had been helpful enough initially, but became fully vested in the cause when the Mossad informed them that not only were the suspected targets of the Muslim extremists variety, but also right-wing extremist American citizens. The U.S. government was particularly sensitive to home-grown terrorist threats, and wanted any information that the Israelis had on this group. The best way for the Americans to obtain this information was to assist the Mossad with this cause.

Yosef was no way so naive as to believe the Americans really cared about this mysterious Jewish artifact he was attempting to protect, but he was no stranger to the *quid pro quo*. In his many years of working within the international intelligence community he had relied upon this same scenario many times himself. He had no problems sharing intel with the Americans about where their domestic skeletons were buried. But, only after they had been of assistance to him.

That is how Yosef became the task force leader of the

agents standing before him. Albeit young, they seemed capable and motivated to assist in a mission they believed was important to American security interests.

"What about the other target?" Yosef asked.

"He was spotted on the security cameras entering the museum, and later approaching Patrick and Hurst in one of the third floor exhibit areas," one of the of young agents said. "However, no one made a live sight identification of him, and a search of the museum has turned up no evidence of him. We'll continue to…"

"Wait," Yosef said suddenly. Something that the agent had said interested him. "You say that Patrick and Hurst had been looking at an exhibit?"

"Yes, sir," the same agent said. "On the third floor."

The mens' discussion was interrupted by the sound of a ringing cell phone. The FBI agent whose phone it was looked slightly embarrassed, but accepted the incoming call.

"Agent Harper," he said simply. "When was that? I'll consult with the lead agent and get back with you on the desired course. Thank you."

He disconnected the call, as the four other men watched him closely.

"Captain Yosef," the young agent named Harper said. "DC Transit Police has video confirmation of Patrick and Hurst entering the Federal Center station. They're believed to now be on a train on the Orange line outbound to Vienna. Should the police move to apprehend?"

Yosef was quiet for several seconds, contemplating.

"No," he said finally. "They're on the path to finding something, and if we intervene too soon we may never find out where that path is leading. I want all of their movements tracked—closely. But, no one is to attempt apprehension until I give the call."

Tom Harper stepped away preparing to make the return call to DC Transit Police HQ.

"Agent Harper," Yosef said calling after him. "The same consideration does not apply to the other target. He is to be apprehended at our earliest opportunity."

Agent Harper nodded in understanding, and continued to move away from the group to make the call.

Tourists continued to stream past them out the exit doors as the museum was now officially closed. None of them were aware of the international intrigue that was taking place directly around them.

Yosef smiled. An expression that none of the agents had seen since first meeting this Mossad captain several hours ago.

"They fly from Pittsburgh, to Spain, then back to Washington all within the span of thirty-six hours. They think they're suspects in a murder they didn't commit, and have recently been pursued by the person they believe is the real murderer."

All of the agents look closely at Namir Yosef, wondering where he was heading with the rehashing of a story they were all briefed on a few hours ago.

"And, yet," Yosef said. "They take the time to seek out one particular exhibit, in one particular museum."

He turns quickly to the most senior FBI agent on his team.

"Find a curator with the museum who can give us some information. And, show me that exhibit that's worthy of a spur-of-the-moment transatlantic flight."

Chapter Forty Two

The train shook and shimmied as it raced forward through the dark tunnels.

Noah Dew was on a Green Line Metro train heading outbound from Washington. He was not sure where he would be going from here, but it did not really matter. At some point in the very near future he would get the upper hand, and he would force the two sodomites to take him to the Holy Light. After that, he would kill them.

He kept repeating the one word in his mind that he had heard them say as he had approached them in the museum.

"*Fischinsel.*"

What did it mean? Was it more Navajo, or possibly some art term? Or, maybe some other language he had never heard? He cringed at the thought that the word may be Yiddish.

He could only assume that it was God's will that he had once again caught up with them and was following their path so closely. He had been very concerned when they had left the United States for Europe that he may have missed his only opportunity to obtain the Holy Light. While he never doubted God's hand in helping him and the church obtain the light, he knew that travel outside of the country without a valid passport would be nearly impossible. However, as always, God had provided him with the correct path.

He had narrowly escaped the "museum of the savages" (as he preferred to think of it) where he had encountered the old Nazi's two boyfriends. There had been a rather serious complication. Noah Dew realized that he was not the only one seeking the two men—there were others in the museum who also sought to intercede with them. He realized that if others were seeking the men, that meant they were also seeking the Holy Light.

Noah Dew had recognized one of the men. Not from sight or previous encounter, but rather by his demeanor and appearance. He was a Jew. More specifically, an agent of the Israeli government. This additional complication greatly concerned Noah Dew, but his faith that God would lead him to the Holy Light was strong and resolute.

He had been pursuing the two men down the staircase of the museum, when he saw the Jew call out to them. They had paused for a few seconds on the second floor landing, then turned from the man and continued running toward the main lobby of the museum.

The Jew had looked up toward Noah Dew's location on the stairs leading to the third floor, and he had quickly ducked behind a pillar to avoid being spotted. He ran down the third floor hallway in the opposite direction until he encountered another stairwell at the end of the hall. He burst through the stairwell doors, and bounded down the steps two at a time.

At the bottom of the stairs, he found a door leading into the first floor lobby and another marked as an emergency exit. He needed to get out of the building quickly, but he feared the attention he would attract if he sounded an alarm. He pushed the door hard, and immediately found himself outside on the South lawn of the museum. To his great relief, no alarm had sounded. God continued to protect him in his quest to find the Holy Light.

He was even more blessed, that when he exited the museum he not only did so by not calling attention to himself, but he exited just in time to see the two sodomites hurrying quickly away from the museum down Third Street.

He pulled a Washington Redskins cap that he had bought earlier in the day, and a sweatshirt out of the knap sack he carried. It was not a great disguise, but he hoped it would be just enough for the two men not to realize that he was on their trail.

He had followed them for a few blocks at a safe distance. They looked around at their surroundings frequently—suspicious and frightened, but yet never seemed to see him. He realized quickly that they were heading toward the Metro station, and he adjusted his pace to continue to maintain a safe distance.

They had boarded an Orange Line train, but had only remained onboard for one stop. At L'Enfant Plaza they had transferred to a Green Line train heading to where the line ended at Greenbelt.

Noah Dew was familiar with this particular line. When he had arrived in DC he had parked his car at the parking facility at the end of the Green Line, and took public transportation into the city. He had originally planned to park at Reagan National, but feared security may be more of an issue there.

He had made a good decision, because it became obvious to him as the train moved further away from the city that they must be now headed to the end of the Green Line as well. Again, he trusted in God, and God continued to guide him on the correct path.

He continued to closely watch the two men from his vantage point two cars back. He could see that they were talking intently. He wish he was closer so that he could hear what they were saying. But, he had a clear view of them, and would be able to quickly follow when they exited the train.

But still, the word continued to swarm in his mind.

Fischinsel.

Chapter Forty Three

The adrenalin rush was beginning to subside somewhat. He was still more frightened than he had ever been in his life, but his heart rate was beginning to return to a pace that could be considered close to normal.

Gabe felt better on the crowded Metro train. Being surrounded by all these people gave him a certain amount of comfort. After all, no one would try anything with all these people around—would they?

Then, of course, he remembered what had happened in the museum. The museum had been full of people, yet not one—but two—of the bad guys had tried to get them in the crowded and busy building. He felt his heart rate begin to climb once again.

He and Kevin were on a Green Line train headed toward the end of the line. They had decided to head there shortly after leaving the museum. Originally they had planned to fly to Columbus, but realized it was impossible to travel by air and still stay under the radar. So, they decided they would rent a car and drive to Columbus instead. Yes, they still would need to show identification to the car rental people, but that mode of travel still offered much greater freedom and anonymity.

Gabe kept thinking about the exhibit Rudy had created at

the Museum of the American Indian. It seemed so random and disconnected, yet he knew that was precisely the point. It was so disconnected and random, that Rudy was clearly trying to send some message to him and Kevin through it.

Kevin looked at Gabe and smiled.

"Thinking about the exhibit at the museum?" he asked.

"How did you know?"

"Well, the look on your face has alternated between near panic and thoughtful contemplation ever since we've been on the train. You look pretty contemplative right now, so I took a guess that you were thinking about the clue instead of the scary men who are chasing us."

Gabe returned the smile.

"I guess I'm pretty transparent, huh?" he said.

"So, what do you think?"

"About the clues in the exhibit, or the scary men?"

"I have a pretty good idea what you think about the scary men. I'm more interested in the clues right now."

"I'm not really sure," Gabe said, turning on the camera on his cell phone to look at the pictures he had taken in the museum. "I think the legend about the raven and the origin of light seems pretty straight forward. 'The warm sphere of light' fits the description of the Tzohar perfectly."

"And," Kevin said. "Everything else in the display also focuses on the subject of light. But, it all seems so disconnected."

"Yeah," Gabe said. "In the main feature we have an Indian legend about how light was created in the universe, mixed in with quotes from an ancient Greek and a Fifteenth Century Brit."

"And, don't forget—dear old Ben Franklin."

"Of course, we can't forget Mr. Franklin," Gabe said sighing. "What do they all have in common? How are they connected?"

"Well, each quote talks about the importance of light," Kevin said.

"Well, technically the Franklin quote talks about a *lighthouse*."

"A fine shade of difference I think," Kevin said.

"But," Gabe said. "A fine shade of a difference could make all the difference when we're talking about Rudy, and what he was trying to tell us."

Kevin nodded silently.

A voice over the loudspeaker interrupted their thoughts, announcing that the train was arriving at the College Park station. Greenbelt—and the end of the line—would be next.

"I also have to think that the letters in bold mean something important."

"Yeah," Kevin said. "But the letters also seemed so random. It doesn't make any sense."

Gabe nodded and glanced at the few people who had joined their train at College Park. Fewer and fewer people boarded the train this far out on the line.

The train then pulled from the station, and continued on to its final stop.

Chapter Forty Four

R obert Wilson Littlefeather was irritated.

He had been sitting in traffic on the Beltway, just a few exits from home, when he received an urgent call from his senior assistant. The FBI was at the museum and needed to speak to him immediately.

He was startled by the call. Why would the FBI be at the museum and need to talk to him so urgently? Had there been some sort of terrorist threat? Nothing like this had ever happened before at the Museum of the American Indian. The worst that usually happened was some pompous congressman demanding a guided tour for some constituent or family member he was trying to impress.

He raced back to the museum in a near panic, fighting rush hour traffic all the way. However, when he arrived he found out that it was not only the FBI who had summoned him, but also an agent with the Israeli intelligence agency. He was incredulous that what they actually wanted to discuss was one of the museum's exhibits.

"Gentlemen," he said, trying to remain as polite as possible. "I don't understand why this could not wait until the museum's regular operating hours."

Robert Littlefeather was the managing director of the museum, and its chief curator. He had worked with the museum since its inception. Actually, well before its inception. A national museum dedicated to the history and culture of his people had been his dream ever since he was a little boy growing up in North Carolina.

He had taken the old family name of Littlefeather, abandoning the anglicized adaptation of "Littleton" that his grandfather had adopted for the family in the 1920s. Robert had never faulted his grandfather for this abandonment of his culture; he was simply trying to make life easier for his children.

As a little boy, he had listened to his grandfather and his friends tell stories of the old ways of their people. He had seen the tears in the old man's eyes as he told the stories of his ancestors. Robert knew that his grandfather had hated having to abandon the family name, and with it—part of his identity. But, he was determined to give his children the best chances for a successful life. And the best way to do that was to try to free them from the label of *Indian*.

Robert's father had married a white woman, who had given birth to Robert and his three brothers. While his maternal grandparents were not initially too pleased with the idea of their little girl marrying a Cherokee, they eventually warmed to their new son-in-law and his family. Robert realized that it could not have been easy for any of them. It was the 1940s, and it was a very different time—especially in the South.

Unlike his brothers, Robert had always embraced his Cherokee heritage. It was not that his brothers were ashamed of their "Indian blood" (as it was most commonly called then), but they just never seemed as interested in it as Robert. He could sit and listen to the stories that his paternal grandfather told by the hour.

He had majored in Native American Studies and Anthropology at the University of Tennessee. It was there that he stopped being Robert Littleton, and formally reclaimed the family name of Littlefeather. If his parents had disapproved of his decision, they never said so. Robert's grandfather died a few months after he had changed his name. He was grateful that the old man had lived to see the family name of Littlefeather live on with him.

Robert spent most of his career teaching Native American history in various colleges around the country, and working with museums on their Native American collections. When an act of congress created the Museum of the American Indian in 1989, Robert was named to head the project. He had been dedicated to the museum ever since.

"Sir," Agent Harper said. "We certainly appreciate your returning to the museum after you were gone for the day, but it is an important matter."

"Ok," Robert Littlefeather said, "but this exhibit has been

here for nearly five years. I'm pretty sure it would still be here tomorrow."

The FBI agents and Namir Yosef ignored the obvious sarcasm of the comment.

"Mr. Littlefeather," Yosef said. "We are looking for some information on this particular exhibit. It may provide some insight into a matter of American and Israeli security."

Robert Littlefeather looked at them with a mixture of surprise and disbelief.

"Can you tell us what it means?"

"Well," Littlefeather said, still somewhat incredulous. "It's based on a Haida legend about the origin of light. It's a popular legend, particularly its parallels to the Christian Bible. You know, 'let there be light.'"

"What about the other panels in the exhibit? They seem somewhat disconnected from the central theme."

"Yes," Littlefeather said. "You're not the first person to mention that. However, when we were fortunate enough to have someone as prestigious as Dr. Zeffner working on a piece, you tend to give him some leeway."

"Dr. Rudolph Zeffner?" Yosef asked.

"Yes," Littlefeather said. "He is one of the foremost experts on religious art in the world."

"*Was* one of the foremost experts. Dr. Zeffner was recently murdered."

"Yes, of course. I heard the horrible news a few days ago. It is a terrible tragedy—a horrible loss for the art history world."

"Did Dr. Zeffner work or consult with anyone else on this particular exhibit?"

"Not that I'm aware of—our collections staff worked only with Rudolph—Dr. Zeffner. Of course, it wouldn't surprise me if he had some graduate students helping on the project, but if so he never mentioned it."

"Did he ever mention about the meaning of the other panels?"

"No," Littlefeather said. "And I asked about it once. The quotes from Plato, Francis Bacon, and Benjamin Franklin—our board had questioned their place in our museum."

"And, what did he say?"

"He explained that the common theme of the exhibit was the connection of light to human spirituality. The importance and meaning of light transcended one culture or nationality—it was reflective of all of human kind."

"And, that was an acceptable answer to you and the museum's board?" the Israeli asked.

"Of course," Littlefeather said. "As I said, when you have someone with the renowned reputation of Rudolph Zeffner working on a project you respect his artistic vision."

Yosef and the other agents nodded in silent understanding.

"So," Littlefeather asked, sensing a change in the mood of the room. "what's so important to the governments of our nations that you have insisted we have discussion this evening?"

"Unfortunately, Mr. Littlefeather," Namir Yosef said. "The exact nature of our work is classified. However, I can tell you that Dr. Zeffner is believed to have had possession of a very important artifact which may have led directly to his murder. We're seeking clues to the whereabouts of that artifact."

Robert Littlefeather looked shocked. Nothing this man was saying made sense to him.

"Thank you for your time, sir. We appreciate your assistance."

Namir Yosef and the other agents turned, and began walking quickly down the exhibit hall away from him. Robert Littlefeather could do nothing but stand and stare as they left him standing alone in front of the *Origin of Light*.

Chapter Forty Five

Interstate 70 meets up with the Pennsylvania Turnpike in the small town of Breezewood, PA—the self-proclaimed "Town of Motels." Breezewood is unique in the lore of the American highway system, in that one mile of the interstate goes directly through Breezewood's surface roads—complete with traffic lights. An odd funding anomaly in the 1960s resulted in Interstate 70 not being directly linked with the Pennsylvania Turnpike, so all traffic must exit the four lane high speed highway and traverse the fast food and motel clogged streets of Breezewood.

This short stretch of road is only one of two locations in the national interstate system where there are traffic lights during the course of an interstate. The situation is so unique that "road geeks" (a self appointed term for those who study public roads as a hobby) refer to any gap in a highway system as a "Breezewood."

The unique configuration of the roadway causes massive traffic jams as the two major highways come together on the streets of Breezewood. While there are no actual residents of the unincorporated town, there are ten motels, over twenty fast food restaurants, and nearly as many gas stations clogging that one mile stretch of road.

Gabe and Kevin had left suburban Maryland over three

hours earlier. They had rented a car at an Avis office near the Greenbelt station, and were making the long drive back to Columbus. Nearly thirty minutes so far had been spent sitting on the clogged stretch of road in Breezewood.

Gabe was not sure what they would actually do when they got back to Columbus. They had followed Rudy's clues from place to place, yet really knew nothing more about the actual location of the Tzohar than they did before. There were a few colleagues left at the university who had worked with both him and Rudy, and he thought they might be able to help them make some sense of the clues. He knew that Rudy had not wanted them to share this secret, but he felt he was running out of other options.

He yawned and rubbed his eyes. The traffic was mind-numbing, and the sun was setting on the horizon and glaring into his eyes. He and Kevin had not spoken much since they left Washington.

"I don't think I can take much more of this," Gabe said.

"The traffic, or this escapade in general?" Kevin asked.

"Well, both actually. But, right now I'm so tired I can barely think straight."

Kevin nodded in agreement. "Is there really any point in killing ourselves to get back to Columbus tonight? We're still going to be just as confused about what to do next tomorrow as we will be tonight."

"So, are you suggesting we stop for the night?"

"Well," Kevin said. "We are in the *Town of Motels*. How often does that happen? It seems a shame not to take advantage of it.

Gabe needed very little convincing, and flipped on his turn signal at the next motel's parking lot. The cracked and fading asphalt led to a low slung one story building motel that did not have more than ten or fifteen units. The green neon vacancy sign flickered in the quickly descending dusk. There were only three other cars in the parking lot.

"I think Norman Bates used to work here," Kevin said with a chuckle.

"Well, at this point I think I could sleep through anything."

"Yeah, me too. But, I think I'll avoid the shower here anyway. But, before any of that I need to get some food. I'm starving."

Kevin pointed across the parking lot to what appeared to be a truck stop. A red neon sign flashed the word *Diner* into the early evening sky. Actually, it flashed *iner*, as the first letter had long since burned out.

"What do you think," Kevin asked. "When in Rome?"

Gabe nodded his head in reluctant agreement, and they turned to walk toward the diner.

Chapter Forty Six

The waitress's hair was bright red, and nearly two feet high in a style that had not been seen in most of the world since the 1970s. However, it still seemed to fit right in Breezewood. She chomped her chewing gum so dramatically, that Gabe was transfixed by watching the constant motion of her jaws.

"So, what's the answer, hon?" she asked, never missing a beat on the gum.

Gabe's hypnosis brought on by the rhythm of the gum chewing came to an abrupt end.

"I'm sorry?"

"What kind of toast, hon? White or wheat?"

"Wheat. Please."

The waitress nodded slightly, scribbled something down on her pad and walked away.

There was something about having breakfast for dinner that had always seemed oddly comforting to him.

"So," Kevin said, once again interrupting Gabe's drifting thoughts. "What do we do now? What exactly do we do when we finally get back to Columbus?"

"That's pretty much all I've thought about since we left the museum. I really think our best bet is to try to get in touch with some of our old friends from the university.

People who knew Rudy."

"But, Rudy didn't want us to get anyone else involved. He made it pretty clear that this was a secret he shared only with us."

Gabe sat back against the vinyl booth and rubbed his eyes with his balled fists.

"Yes, Kevin, I realize that. But I'm pretty much out of ideas at this point. I don't know anything else to do."

Kevin nodded. While he did not like the answer, he knew that he also lacked any better ones. He picked up Gabe's cell phone that sat on the table between them, and launched its photo viewer.

"Well," Kevin said. "Let's take another look at our most recent clue."

He stared closely at the few photos Gabe had been able to snap before they had been approached by the tattooed man in the museum.

"*Fischinsel,*" he said. "I think it sounds German."

Gabe stopped rubbing his eyes and looked directly at Kevin.

"*Fish island,*" he said.

"What?"

"*Fischinsel* in German would roughly translate to *fish island* in English."

"Fish island?" Kevin asked. "Is that a place?"

Gabe reached over to the messenger bag that sat on the diner booth next to him, and pulled out his laptop. He booted it up and was relieved to find that in this day and age, the pervasiveness of wireless internet had even found its way to Breezewood.

He clicked into the search web site, and entered *fischinsel* and *fish island*, then clicked the search button. The search only returned ten results, but what caught Gabe's eye was the entry at the top of the page:

Did you mean: fischerinsel fish island

He clicked on the provided link, and was taken to a new page with a few hundred results. All of which referred to an area called Fischerinsel located in one of the oldest parts of Berlin.

"There's an area of Berlin called Fischerinsel, or Fisherman's Island. It's one of the oldest parts of Berlin and dates back to the thirteenth century."

"Well, Rudy was always attracted to places with a sense of history."

"There's more. It's in the neighborhood of what is today a very important museum district in Berlin."

"Bingo," Kevin said. "That has Rudy written all over it."

Gabe nodded in agreement.

"It was originally the home of wealthy ship builders and seafarers, but by the seventeenth century it had become pretty much a ghetto."

I have always striven to honor the fishermen.

Gabe continued to scan the various web sites returned in his search.

"Most of the original area was destroyed during World War Two. During the sixties and seventies, the whole area was rebuilt with high rise apartments. Only one medieval structure still survives—something called the *Friedrichs-gracht* house."

"Didn't Rudy's clue in Spain say something about fisher-men?" Kevin asked.

"Yes. *I have always striven to honor the fisherman.*"

"So," Kevin said. "We have a clue in Spain talking about the importance of fisherman, and a clue in Washington spelling out Fisherman's Island..."

"Well, sort of," Gabe said.

"What?"

"The clue in the museum actually spelled out *fischinsel*, or *fish island*. Google made the leap to Fischerinsel for us."

"Yeah, ok. But, it's a fine shade of difference if you ask me."

Gabe nodded in half-hearted agreement, but said nothing.

"Plus," Kevin continued. "In this same neighborhood we've got one centuries-old structure surrounded by a sea of high rises. You know how Rudy felt about the preservation of historical buildings. Can you think of a hiding place that he'd prefer more?"

Gabe nodded again.

"This just all fits together too well not to be the answer."

"Yeah," Gabe said. "I agree. It all fits."

Gabe tapped a few commands on the laptop, and within a few minutes he was checking on flight availability to Berlin.

"There's a flight out of Pittsburgh that leaves tomorrow afternoon. That would be perfect, considering my car has been in long term parking there since we went to Spain."

He tapped in a few more commands.

"It looks like there's only three seats left on that flight, and after that the next availability isn't until Monday. I'm going to book it."

"Is that a good idea?" Kevin asked. "Based on our experience at the museum, it's pretty clear that there are people still looking for us. Should we make it that easy to follow our trail?"

"I can hold the tickets with just a name until Noon tomorrow without purchasing them. Then, we'll just pay cash for them at the airport. Maybe we won't raise anyone's attention without any credit card activity."

"I guess we really don't have any other choice," Kevin said.

"Finish up your French Toast, I'm about ready to fall asleep sitting here."

Feeling satisfied that they finally had the next step in place, they finished the rest of the meal in silence.

Chapter Forty Seven

Gabe and Kevin walked across the parking lot from the Diner (or, "iner" as Gabe now preferred to think of it) to the motel building. A sign reading *Office*, and looking as though it had been around since the Second World War, hung in the glass door.

A bell hanging on the inside of the door jam announced their arrival. A woman who looked to be in her mid sixties came from a small room behind the front desk. Her name tag simply read *JoAnn*.

"May I help you?" she asked.

"Yes, we were just looking for a room for the night," Gabe replied.

The older lady looked at Gabe for a second, then turned her gaze toward Kevin.

"Just one room?" she asked, overly emphasizing the word *one*.

"Yep," Gabe replied. "That's what I want."

He was exhausted, and was really in no mood to deal with this woman's 1950s ideal of morality. She could think what she wanted to think—he was beyond the point of caring.

"Ok, that will be forty seven dollars with tax," she said in a flat tone.

Kevin pulled out a fifty dollar bill out of his pocket and handed it to her.

"Keep the change, ma'am," he said smiling, and tipping an imaginary hat.

The woman seemed amused by Kevin's comment, and returned the smile. He always knew just when to turn on the charm, Gabe thought. He had to give him that.

The woman handed Kevin a room key, and he and Gabe turned to walk out of the lobby.

"You boys have a good night. But, *not too good*," she said laughing.

Gabe rolled his eyes, but continued walking. He heard Kevin chuckle behind him, and ignored it.

＊ ＊ ＊ ＊

Gabe and Kevin were both sound asleep within fifteen minutes of entering their room. Kevin had not even bothered to turn down the covers on his double bed.

If they would have stayed awake a few minutes longer, they may have heard the room door next to their's open and close. But, the occupant of that room had very little intention of sleeping.

Noah Dew leaned up against the internal door connecting his room to his target's and listened. He would listen all night long if necessary. No amount of physical discomfort would stop him from fulfilling his destiny.

Chapter Forty Eight

G abe's head had barely hit the pillow before he was asleep.

His head swirled in darkness. He looked all around him, but all he could see in every direction was more nothingness. He heard a noise behind him, and he turned quickly in the direction of the sound. Still, he could see nothing.

Suddenly above him was the form of a giant black bird. In its mouth was a glowing orb that was rapidly changing colors; from blue, to red, to green, to yellow and back to blue again. Gabe could feel an electric-like energy radiating from the orb.

"Tzohar," he whispered.

The large black bird flew toward him, and he could see its razor sharp talons bearing down on him. He tried to scream, but no sound would escape his lips. He dove into the ground, trying to evade the bird.

He looked up, and there was nothing but darkness again. As quickly as it had appeared, the bird—and the orb it carried—were gone. Once again, only darkness surrounded him.

Liebchen.

At first he was not sure if he had actually heard the word. He strained his ears trying to hear.

Liebchen.

He was sure he heard it this time. He turned toward the

direction of the sound. He saw a warm glow, somewhat like a spotlight, begin to form in the distance. He stared at the light. He saw Rudy looking back at him.

"Liebchen," Rudy said again softly.

"Rudy, is that you? We thought you were dead."

"No one really dies, Liebchen. Not if there is someone still around to remember them."

Gabe smiled. He had forgotten that Rudy was fond of that expression.

"You are missing the path."

"What? What do you mean?"

"You are thinking too literally. As I always tried to teach you—sometimes it was ok to be literal, but sometimes a problem requires less concrete thought. Freud may have said 'sometimes a banana is just a banana', but sometimes the banana may actually look like something else."

"Rudy, we've tried our hardest. We must be missing something—some clue we've overlooked."

"No, liebchen. You have missed nothing. You must now just put them all together."

The light began to fade, and Rudy along with it. Gabe tried to move toward him, but before he could, he was gone.

✳ ✳ ✳ ✳

Gabe could hear Kevin's voice in the distance. Startled, he opened his eyes. Kevin was standing over him, staring down at him.

"Something's wrong," Kevin said. "I think we're on the wrong path."

Chapter Forty Nine

G abe felt as though he was quickly ascending from the depths of a very deep pool as he became awake. His eye lids fluttered as he struggled to open them. The sounds of Kevin's voice had roused him from the very deep, very real dream.

The heavy blackout curtains in the motel room window were drawn, but bright sunlight shone through the small separation where the two panels did not quite come together. The glare of the light was directly in Gabe's eye.

"There's something wrong," Kevin said again. "This doesn't make sense."

After his dream, Gabe understood exactly what Kevin meant, but still he felt the need for him to explain—if only to help him better understand his own thoughts. He wondered if Kevin had dreamt of Rudy as well.

"In all the time that you knew Rudy," Kevin continued. "Did you ever know him to go back to Germany? Even once?"

"No, not even once. In fact, it was almost impossible to even get him to talk about Germany."

"Exactly," Kevin said. "He told me once that there were too many painful memories there. So, why in the world would he choose that place to stash what he considered to be the greatest treasure in the history of the world?"

"He wouldn't," Gabe said. Suddenly, the dream of Rudy seemed much clearer and made much more sense.

Gabe got out of bed, and quickly walked to the luggage valet by the wall. He began digging frantically through his bag, tossing things onto the floor. Finally, he pulled out the bottle of wine left for them in Spain, and held it up to Kevin.

"Does this picture on the wine bottle look familiar to you?"

Kevin squinted in the still near dark room. A look of knowing realization came over his face.

"The museum!" Kevin said. "The raven on the wine label is the same as the one in Rudy's exhibit in the Indian museum!"

"Yes, I believe it is," Gabe said. "it also says the wine is from the islands of Lake Erie. So, we have the mention of an island on the wine bottle, and the spelling out of *fischinsel*—or *fish island*—in the museum."

"A bass is a fish," Kevin said quietly.

Gabe looked at him, unsure of where this train of thought was heading.

"True," Gabe said less patiently than he intended. "And, a raven is a bird. Are you telling me you know of some place called Bass Island?"

"There are actually three Bass Islands—all in Lake Erie,"

Kevin said. "North Bass, Middle Bass, and South Bass. South Bass is the most famous."

Gabe's eyes widened with this new information.

"And what makes you such an expert on islands in Lake Erie?"

"I spent a lot of time up there. I spent every Summer when I was an undergrad working at Cedar Point. My friends and I used to go out to the islands all the time."

"So, did Rudy ever mention anything to you about the Bass Islands?"

Kevin seemed to think for a moment, then a broad smile came across his face.

"What? What is it?"

"Well, Rudy never mentioned the islands exactly. But, he mentioned the South Bass Lighthouse several times."

"A lighthouse?" Gabe asked, his voice rising.

"Yep. The South Bass Lighthouse is located on South Bass Island. It's actually owned by Ohio State and used as a research and office facility."

"Really? Did Rudy ever visit there?"

"Did he ever mention a Peter Flynn to you?"

"Peter Flynn? Of course. He was one of the few ex-boyfriends that Rudy stayed friends with. I think they had a brief thing back in the 70s. Rudy always joked that Peter was the only man of science who ever interested him."

"Yeah, that's him—nice guy. He visited us in Dallas a few years ago. But, the interesting thing for us now is his job."

"His job?"

"Yes—he's the chair of the environmental studies department that runs the Lake Erie research facilities. He oversees the lighthouse, and from the conversations he and Rudy had, they had spent quite a bit of time there over the years."

Rudy's voice rang in Gabe's head. *You have missed nothing. You must now just put them all together.*

"Are you thinking what I'm thinking?"

"Well, I'm thinking that maybe lighthouses really are more useful than churches," Kevin said smiling.

"My thoughts exactly. I knew there was a reason that Franklin was my favorite of the founding fathers."

"So, I guess we know our next step now. It's probably about a five hour drive from here up to the lake, then about another hour on a boat out to the island."

Gabe looked at the clock on the bedside table.

"I can't believe how late it is! We were asleep for like fifteen hours!"

"I know," Kevin replied. "We better get a move on. None of the public ferries are operating out to the islands right now, but I'm pretty sure I know where we can get our hands on a boat."

✳ ✳ ✳ ✳

Gabe and Kevin began packing up what few belongings they had with them, and within ten minutes were heading out the door of the motel room.

An unblinking eye watched them through the peep hole of the room next door as they walked to the parking lot, and tossed their belongings into the car. Noah Dew would wait a few minutes before heading out to his own car and continuing the pursuit.

He could not believe how fortunate he was. Both for the paper-thin motel walls, and for God directing the two sodomites to reveal all the answers to him.

Once again, the men were revealing the path to him. This time to an island in the middle of Lake Erie—and to the Holy Light. This time he was certain that he would be the only one coming back.

Chapter Fifty

The drive that should have taken five hours or less ended up taking nearly seven and a half. There had been road construction around the I-70/77 interchange, then they had hit rush hour traffic as they got closer to Cleveland.

It was nearly seven-thirty when they pulled into the gravel parking lot in front of a dilapidated building on the outskirts of Sandusky, OH. A sign with chipped and faded paint hung over the door. It read *Pete's Bait and Boat Excursions*.

Gabe looked around at the rusting shells of boats sitting around the yard. He could only discern a gulf of darkness behind the one story building, and beyond that small lights very far in the distance. He assumed he was looking across Sandusky Bay.

"So, With all the nice boat yards we passed on the drive out to this place, do you want to explain why this is the one you picked?"

"Well, it's kind of a long story. But, let's just say that Pete and I go back a long way."

Gabe looked at him skeptically.

"Back during those Summers when I worked at Cedar Point, my friends and I used to have Pete buy beer for us."

"That's real responsible. So, we're going to rent a boat

from a guy who actively participated in contributing to the delinquency of minors."

"Well, Pete didn't do it for nothing—there was a certain *quid-pro-quo* expected."

Gabe raised one eye brow and gave Kevin a sly grin.

"We used to call him 'Pete the Perv.' Pete expected to see a little skin in exchange for making the buy at the liquor store."

"Gross," Gabe said.

"Yeah, it's amazing what you'll do when you're nineteen and you and your friends want to party. I think some of the guys might have gone a little farther sometimes—depending on how uncooperative Pete was being."

Again, Gabe gave Kevin the same raised eyebrow look.

Kevin playfully punched him in the upper arm.

"Well, not me! I never wanted a beer that bad."

Gabe's smile widened. Kevin rolled his eyes.

"Ok, let's get this over with," Kevin said, opening the car door.

They walked across the gravel parking lot. Only faint light was visible from within the building, most of which seemed to be generated from a soda machine just inside the door. The buzz of the florescent street lights in the parking lot seemed exceedingly loud in the otherwise quiet cool night air. As they got closer, they could see that a hand-made sign reading *Closed* was hanging on the inside of the door.

"Great, he's closed. What are we going to do now?"

"Pete will be here," Kevin said, continuing toward the door. "He lives here."

Kevin walked up to the door and rang the buzzer on the side. They could hear the loud ringing coming from within the building. Kevin waited a second, then pushed the button a second time. Then a third. Finally, he just leaned on the button and continued to let it blare.

Gabe's eye caught an additional light come on in a room further back within the building. A few seconds later, he saw a large man stumble into the doorway separating that room from the main area of the store.

Even at his best, Pete Polasky was not what one would consider a handsome man. But, Pete was far from his best. His face carried about a three days growth of beard, which was an odd mixture of the bright red hair of his youth and his current grey. He was wearing a tee shirt which was supposed to be white, and a pair of old blue sweatpants with a University of Michigan emblem. He had a three-quarter empty bottle of Southern Comfort in his hand hanging at his side.

He squinted as he looked to see who was ringing the bell at his door.

"Can't you fellas fuckin' read?" he yelled. "The sign says I'm fuckin' closed!"

"Pete," Kevin shouted to him from the other side of the door. "It's Kevin Hurst. We were…" he hesitated for a moment. "*Friends*—a few years back. Do you remember me?"

Pete continued to stare, and squinted trying to remember the man calling to him. He walked closer to the door, and continued to stare down Kevin. A look of drunken recognition crossed his face, and he smirked. He flipped the dead bolt, unlocking the outside door.

"Fuck, Kevin. I wouldn't exactly say that we was *friends*," Pete said, badly slurring the last word. "No, I'd say you were a little cock tease who needed me to buy him beer to get trashed with his equally cock tease buddies."

"Yeah," Kevin said attempting to laugh. "That's probably true, but that was a long time ago, Pete."

Kevin's attempt at brevity had little impact on Pete's demeanor.

"So, aren't you old enough to buy beer for yourself yet? Or, is that what this guy is for?" Pete said, motioning toward Gabe with his hand holding the whiskey bottle. Gabe forced a sick smile, and tried to ignore the whiskey spilled on his shoes.

"No, Pete. This is my friend Gabe. And, we're here because we need to rent a boat."

"A boat? Tonight?" Pete asked incredulously. "It's dark

and the season is long over. There's a reason the tourist ferries don't run this time of year, Einstein."

"Yeah, I understand that. But this is really important—we have to get out to South Bass tonight."

Pete shook his head, and held the door open and motioned for Kevin and Gabe to enter the store.

"Well, if you want a boat from me tonight you better be ready to give me a little more than a peek at your cock," Pete said, obscenely enunciating the last word.

Kevin swallowed and smiled nervously.

"Don't worry, boy," Pete said laughing. "You're a little past my prime age now. I don't want your ass anymore—I want cash."

Gabe was sure he could see a look of genuine relief spread across Kevin's face.

"Sir," Gabe said, speaking for the first time to Pete. "I think we can make a very fair offer for rental of one of your boats."

He pulled out a large wad of cash from his inside jacket pocket. For what seemed to be the hundredth time in the last few days, he was grateful that Rudy had had the foresight to leave them so much cash for this quest.

"There's five thousand dollars here. It all belongs to you for just letting us use one of your boats for a few hours."

Pete's eyes grew wide, and he licked his lips.

"You assholes are fuckin' nuts," Pete said, reaching out to snatch the money from Gabe's hand. "But, my daddy always said a nut's money spends just as easy." He laughed heartily, and the wet sound made both Gabe and Kevin feel slightly nauseated.

"Now, I don't do quite as much business as I used to when you were around here, Kevin," Pete said walking back toward his rental counter. "Times are hard, so my boats might not be up to the standards of you and your sugar daddy here," he motioned his thumb toward Gabe. "But, you'll have to take it or leave it."

He reached behind the desk and pulled out a set of keys on a Pepsi key ring. He handed the key ring to Kevin.

"She's not real pretty, or real fast, but she'll get you out to South Bass and back. Most likely."

"That's all we're looking for," Kevin said, taking the keys from Pete.

"She's in slip number seven around back. Just put the keys in the night drop box when you get back. I don't plan on you waking me up again."

"Thanks, Pete—we really appreciate it," Kevin said, extending his hand.

Pete looks down at Kevin's hand, and pushed it away.

"So now I get to touch you, huh?" Pete snarled. "Forget it. You boys just get the fuck out of my store."

Kevin shrugged his shoulders, and motioned to Gabe to move toward the door. They quickly exited the building and into the chilly night. They heard Pete flip the dead bolts and lock the door behind them.

Noah Dew stepped back into the shadows near the side of the cinder block building, when Patrick and Hurst came out of the building into the parking lot. He had parked his car a block down the street so as not to alert them to his presence.

The men had been inside the building for less than ten minutes, and when they exited they headed around to the boat dock. Obviously, they had chosen this place to procure a boat for the trip out to Bass Island.

Noah Dew felt that if the sodomites could talk the proprietor of Pete's Marina into providing them with a boat, he could easily do the same. After all, Noah Dew could be very persuasive when he needed to be.

Chapter Fifty One

Peter "Pete" Polasky stumbled into the back room that served as his office, bedroom, living room, and kitchen. He shook his head in disbelief. He could not believe that the little punk had shown up again here after all this time.

Over the years, he had bought lots of beer for under-age boys. It was funny how the word spread from season to season among the kids who worked the summers out on Cedar Point. Every May, a new group of them would show up at his door. He was an easy mark, and all they had to do was give him a little peek. Sometimes he was able to talk them into going a little further, especially when they had already consumed some of the beer he had bought.

But, that Kevin kid had been different. Sure he wanted beer and had showed him some skin—just like all the others—but he had also actually talked to Pete. He had treated him like a real person, instead of just some freak that they had to drop their pants in front of for a six pack.

His thoughts were interrupted by the ringing at the door again.

"There's no fucking way I'm giving that money back," Pete said to no one in particular.

He walked into the doorway separating his living area from the front of the store. He could see someone standing at the glass door, but he could not see who it was. He was pretty sure it was not Kevin or his friend—this person seemed much taller and as thin as a rail.

"Who the hell is it," he shouted toward the door. "Can't you see that I'm closed? Apparently nobody can fucking read tonight."

"Sir," the tall man responded in a southern accent. "I'm in a desperate situation, and I need your help."

He then said something else that Pete could not quite make out. He stepped further into the store and closer to the door.

"I ain't no damn Mother Teresa," Pete said. "There's a 7-11 down the road, they can help you there."

"I'm in dire need of a boat," the man said. Again, he said something else that was inaudible.

Pete stepped even closer to the door. From this vantage point he could see the man much clearer. He was over six feet tall, and maybe weighed one-fifty soaking wet. He had a short crew cut, and tattoos covering both arms. Despite the evening cold, he was wearing just a tee shirt. Pete thought the tats looked homemade—he had seen plenty of similar ink during his years in the Navy.

"Buddy, my last rental just went out. The only boat I have left is my own personal craft, and I sure as hell ain't loaning it out. Come back tomorrow, and I'll see what I can do for you then. Go on and get out of here."

Pete was trying his best to sound gruff, but his voice cracked on the last word. There was something about this stranger at his door that really scared him.

"I'm sorry you feel that way," Noah Dew said quietly, and reached into the waist band of his jeans.

Pete's eyes grew wide when he saw the glint of the gun in the parking lot lights.

"You're fucking crazy," he screamed, diving behind the counter. He landed hard on his knee. He was pretty sure that he had broken his knee cap in the dive, but that was the least of his worries right now.

Noah Dew shot at the door handle, blowing away the glass and a good part of the metal door frame. He reached through the broken door glass, and flipped open the dead bolt. He stepped into the store, the broken glass crunching beneath his feet.

Pete Polasky lay behind the desk, his heart pounding in his chest. At first he was unsure of what the strange noise around him was, but then realized it was the sound of his own frantic sobbing. His heart pounded in his chest, and a sharp pain was radiating from his left arm. He realized that this must be what having a heart attack felt like.

Noah Dew walked behind the desk, and stood over him. He pointed the gun directly at his face.

"All you had to do was give me a boat," Noah Dew said. "That was all you had to do."

"I'm ssssorry," Pete said sobbing. "The keys are on the desk. Take it—take it. Just please leave me alone."

Noah Dew looked at the blubbering mess laying on the floor below him. The fat, drunken slob disgusted him. He spit into the man's face. For a moment, his sobbing increased and he put his hand to his face, frantically wiping away the spit as if it were burning him.

"Please. Please—leave me alone. I think I'm having a heart attack," he cried.

Noah Dew glared down at him. *Pathetic*, he thought.

"Then," Noah Dew said almost gently. "I'll do the Christ-like thing. I'll do you the favor of putting you out of your misery." He cocked the gun.

Pete's eyes grew wider, and he struggled to crawl out of range of the gun pointing down at him, but the only motion he could accomplish was flopping on the floor like a beached fish.

Noah Dew fired two shots directly into Peter Polasky's brain. Within seconds of firing, he literally saw the life leave the man's eyes.

He's gone to a better place than he deserves, he thought.

He picked up a large ring of keys from the desk, and turned and walked out of the store and into the parking lot.

And, as quickly as he had entered Peter Polasky's life—he was gone.

Chapter Fifty Two

Gabe stared at the boat in front of them. He quickly looked around to see if there were any other alternatives.

"Are you sure that's it?" Gabe asked incredulously.

"Yeah," Kevin answered. "I'm afraid that is it."

"Are you sure that it's safe? We've got to go half way to Canada in that thing, and it looks like it could fall apart before it gets a hundred yards from the dock."

"I'm sure it will be fine. Older boats always look a little rough. It comes from sitting out in the weather all the time."

Gabe did not say anything in response. He did not believe that explanation for a second, but he knew Kevin was trying to make him feel more confident. He decided not to argue the point. After all, it was not like they had a lot of other options available to them.

The manufacturer's plate on the boat indicated that it was a Bayliner Capri manufactured in 1985. Gabe did not know a lot about nautical craft, but he estimated it to be somewhere between fifteen and twenty feet long. There was no cabin or indoor area to the boat—only bench seats and a canvas awning over the controls. It would be a cold night out on the lake.

"Do you know how to get to Bass Island?" Gabe asked.

"It seems like a small speck of land in the middle of the lake might be easy to miss?"

"We boated out there about a hundred times during the Summers I worked at the park."

"Yeah, no offense—but that's been more than a few years ago, Kevin."

"Well," Kevin said smiling. "I thought of that. That's why I brought this with us." Kevin held up a mobile GPS device. "This should get us there in the darkest of nights."

"Where did you get that?"

"I took it out of the rental car. They had it secured in there pretty good, but I was able to pull it out without too many scratches."

"Kevin!" Gabe exclaimed. "You're not supposed to remove that from the rental car. It's in the contract."

"Yeah," Kevin said rolling his eyes. "And that's certainly our biggest problem right now, isn't it?"

"I guess I'm just really starting to question the wisdom of setting sail when it's this dark. Maybe we should just wait until first thing in the morning."

"The longer we wait, the more likely those guys from Washington will catch back up with us. Let's face it Gabe, we're in some deep shit here. Real or not, these people think the Tzohar exists and they're after it—and by association—us!"

Gabe considered Kevin's words. "Yeah, you're right. We have no choice—we need to do this tonight."

Gabe stepped off the dock and onto the stern of the boat. "Ok sailor," he said smiling. "So, show me how this thing works."

Kevin returned the smile, and gave him a mock salute.

"It's been a long time since a man called me *sailor*. But, notice I didn't say the first time." Gabe returned the smile, grateful once again for Kevin's ability to bring levity into a very stressful situation.

Kevin untied the boat from the dock and tossed the rope to Gabe. He caught it and pulled it into the body of the craft. Kevin gave the boat a shove, and as it backed away from the slip, Kevin jumped from the dock onto the boat's stern.

Kevin settled in behind the controls. It took a few tries to get the engine started, but finally the inboard engine roared to life. Kevin put the engine in reverse and backed away from the dock. Once he got several yards away, he put the boat into low gear and headed out of the harbor into the open lake.

Within a few minutes, they realized it was even colder out on the lake than either one of them had thought it would be. Gabe searched through the storage bins under the padded bench seats.

"There's a couple of old blankets in here. They don't smell real great though."

"Yeah, thanks but no thanks," Kevin said. "Knowing Pete, I sort of hate to think where those blankets may have been."

"Good point," Gabe said, tossing the blankets back into the storage bins, and quickly wiping his hands on his pants.

Neither one said anything else for at least the next fifteen minutes. There was only a sliver of moon tonight, and the lake was black ink. Luckily, the night was still and the water was very calm. That was unusual for this time of year.

The sound of the boat's engines roared in Gabe's ears. The spotlight on the front of the boat lit the lake in front of them, but still Gabe doubted if they could see one hundred feet of what lay in front. If there was any debris in their path they would ram into it long before Kevin had a chance to react.

Gabe turned to look toward the water behind the boat. For just a second, he was sure he had heard something behind them. He listened closely—nothing. Then, a few seconds later he thought he heard it again.

He reached back into the storage bin beneath the padded seats and pulled out the flash light he had seen earlier, but carefully avoiding the suspect blankets. He turned it on, the light was dim but he smacked the side of the flashlight a few times and it brightened slightly. He turned it toward the empty water trailing behind their boat, but he could only see maybe twenty feet behind them.

Kevin turned back to look at him. "What are you doing?" he asked.

"I could have sworn I heard something. I thought some-one might be following us."

Kevin turned and looked back behind them. He strained to listen, but heard nothing.

"I don't hear anything. You must have heard the echo of the boat's engine on the lake. It's flat so sound really car-ries out here."

Gabe nodded, but Kevin could tell he was not completely convinced.

"I'm really sure it was nothing. We're both a little on edge, but there's no way those guys from Washington could have tracked us down this quickly. We were very careful not to leave a trail."

Gabe nodded in agreement, but still said nothing.

They had been in the water about forty-five minutes when Gabe saw lights in the distance.

"Is that it?" he asked.

"Yes," Kevin replied. "That's actually the lights from Put-in-Bay we can see from the far side of the island. There's probably only about 150 people total on the island this time of year. Compared to about ten thousand on a typical Summer weekend."

Kevin powered down the motor, and maneuvered the boat around the south tip of the island. The South Bass Island lighthouse was no longer used as a functional lighthouse, but still contained a light in the upper tower. It was mostly for ornamental purposes.

Gabe was surprised when Kevin announced that it was the lighthouse in front of them. He had expected a typical New England-esque lighthouse, with the white obelisk and rotating light at the top. However, this one more closely resembled a large house than the stereotypical edifice.

It was built in the late 1800s, in a style that could best be described as "Victorian mansion." The main part of the red brick building consisted of two main floors, a basement and an attic. A square tower at one corner of the building rose two additional stories, and was topped by a circular wooden white cap that had housed the lamp.

"That's it?" Gabe asked. "It doesn't even really look like a lighthouse. It looks more like a house. And, a haunted house at that."

"Yeah, most people don't even realize it's a lighthouse. It's got a really interesting history too. One of the early light keepers actually went insane during a smallpox scare on the island and killed himself by jumping from the tower."

"Yeah, sounds really great," Gabe said. "Not that stumbling around in a dark building wasn't going to be exciting enough, now we can keep an eye out for smallpox guy's ghost as well."

Kevin completely killed the motor and let the boat drift toward a small dock behind the lighthouse. When the craft was close enough, he threw the rope around a post on the dock. He jumped from the boat to the wooden dock and tightly tied off the rope.

"Ok," Kevin said. "I guess it's time to get this show on the road. The quicker we find the damn magical rock, the quicker we can get this nightmare behind us."

Gabe nodded, and followed Kevin off the boat. They started walking up the hill toward the lighthouse, which other than the decorative light in the tower, was completely dark.

Offshore and in the darkness, out of sight range of Gabe and Kevin, Noah Dew sat in his silent boat on the calm lake and watched them walk.

Chapter Fifty Three

Kevin trudged up the grassy bank from the boat dock with Gabe following closely behind. A large sign at the edge of the lighthouse's yard gave full and clear notice that the property was under the jurisdiction of The Ohio State University, and trespassing was strictly prohibited.

"Do you think there's anyone here?" Gabe asked.

"I really doubt it at this time of year. The university mostly uses the lighthouse for offices and Summer housing for students working in the environmental labs. I don't think anyone wants to take the risk of being stuck out on this island when the first snow hits."

There were some external security lights in the yard and on both the front and back porches, but other than that the building appeared to be dark.

"Did you bring the flashlight with you from the boat?" Kevin asked.

"Yeah, have it in my jacket pocket."

"Good, because it looks like we're going to need it."

The windows on the first floor were about six feet off the ground, and would be too hard to try to enter from the yard. Both porches were well lit, and even though the island was mostly deserted, it did not seem wise to put themselves on what was essentially a lighted stage while they were breaking and entering. With few other options, Kevin walked to the back of the house and began examining the basement windows.

"I think this makes the most sense for a point of entry," Kevin said.

Gabe nodded in agreement. He did not relish the idea of crawling around in a dark cellar, but he agreed there were no other real options.

After checking several, Kevin finally found a basement window with a broken latch near the back porch. He pushed on it, careful to pull his sleeves down over his hands. (Both to avoid the glass shards if the window should break, and to limit the number of fingerprints he and Gabe left.) The window resisted at first, but then gave way and opened.

"Hand me the flashlight," he said to Gabe.

Kevin shone the flashlight through the open window, reflecting against the dirt cellar floor below.

"It looks like it's only a six foot or so drop—it shouldn't be too hard."

He handed the flashlight back to Gabe, and swung his legs through the open window. Sliding on his back, he shimmied his body further into the window. When he was over half way in, gravity took over and he fell the rest of way through the window. He hit the hard floor below with a thump.

"Well," Kevin shouted out to Gabe. "It might be a little more than six feet."

Gabe reached in through the window and handed the flashlight to Kevin. He then followed his lead, and within a few seconds also found himself on the cellar floor.

"Yeah, that's more like ten feet if you ask me."

"Well, we're in now, and haven't set off any alarms. So I consider that a limited success so far."

Gabe turned on the flashlight, and was immediately dismayed by how dim the light seemed. He smacked the side of the flashlight a few times, and as it had out on the boat, it brightened slightly. He moved the light around their immediate surroundings, but saw nothing more than boxes and cobwebs. In the opposite corner of their point of entry was a wooden staircase leading to a closed door.

"Looks like that's where we need to go."

Gabe and Kevin slowly climbed the stairs. The creaking of the old wood seemed to echo unbearably against the cellar walls. From all indications, the lighthouse building appeared to be completely void of all human life other than them, but still, the noise so clearly announcing their presence was disconcerting.

When they reached the top of the stairs, Kevin—still concerned with leaving fingerprints—pulled his sleeves down over his hand before he turned the door knob. The door slowly opened, and creaked even louder than the stairs.

Kevin stepped out into the main floor of the lighthouse building, and looked around carefully with the flashlight.

"We need to keep an eye out for motion detectors, or any other kind of security system," Kevin said. "It's not like there's a big police force on the island—but, still."

The first floor of the building seemed to be set up as office space. Gabe noticed the familiar Ohio State property tags on a variety of furniture and office equipment. The building felt too cold to have anyone regularly inhabiting it. Gabe figured they kept the heat at minimal levels during the off-season.

They walked toward the main door of the building which led in from the front porch, and encountered another staircase. This one looking much more substantial than the one that had led them from the basement. Kevin pointed the flashlight up the length of the stairs. Beyond the landing of the second floor, the stairs continued onward.

"It looks like these stairs lead all the way to the attic," Kevin said.

"What about the light tower?" Gabe asked.

"It's in the corner of the building, so it most likely has it's own staircase leading up into the tower from the main structure."

Gabe nodded. He realized that he was somewhat surprised at Kevin's demeanor. He seemed confident—and responsible. Gabe realized that he had changed a lot over the past several years. He tried to ascribe exactly the feeling he was having about Kevin right now, and realized that the only description that really fit was *pride*. He smiled to himself.

"What's so funny?" Kevin asked.

"Nothing at all—just never figured you'd be leading me through a dark lighthouse. Let's keep moving."

They followed the main staircase to the third floor attic, skipping the second floor entirely. The attic was one large open space stretching the entire length of the main building. The walls sloped with the rise of the roof, with the center reaching to about an eight foot ceiling height.

The attic was mostly empty, with the exception of some boxes with the university logo on them. The space was very dusty and covered in cobwebs. It was obvious that the attic had not been used in quite some time. Kevin swept the space with the flashlight. He and Gabe were both startled when a pair of red eyes confronted them. A large rat went scurrying off into a pile of boxes.

"Well, I see the university still doesn't believe in budgeting much for exterminators," Gabe said.

Kevin continued to sweep the rapidly dimming flashlight around the attic. The light caught something large in the far corner. Kevin directed the light beam on it, and saw that it was a metal spiral staircase leading upward.

"That's got to be the stairs to the light tower," he said.

They made their way to the spiral stairs and began to climb upward. The staircase climbed past two additional landings which were merely wide spaces with windows that looked out onto the grounds below. The staircase terminated in the rounded top of the tower.

The round tower was about eight feet high, and had floor to ceiling windows along all sides. Through the windows, Gabe could see the inky blackness of the lake stretching out before them. On the other side, he could see the village lights of Put-in-Bay, and the obelisk tower of the Commodore Perry Peace Monument.

In the center of the circular room was a large raised casing holding what was now purely a decorative light fixture. In the days when this was an actual functioning lighthouse, the output from the light would have been too bright for them to bear. But now, only a mild eerie yellow glow illuminated the tower room. Other than the light, the room was completely empty.

"There's nothing here," Kevin said crestfallen. "There's not a damn thing here."

"Ok," Gabe said, picking up on Kevin's rising frustration. "Let's just stop and think for a minute. We know Rudy wouldn't just leave it laying wide out in the open."

"I can't believe this—it's not fucking here. It's not fucking here! This was our only chance to get out of this mess. No one is going to believe our story now."

Gabe cringed as Kevin kicked the metal base which held the light. The base which held the light shook wildly. Kevin kicked it again. The light flickered briefly, then went dark. The only light remaining in the tower was the fading bulb of the flashlight.

"Kevin…" Gabe whispered.

"I really don't care if I broke the damn thing, Gabe," he said sharply.

"No, it's not that—*look*"

Kevin noticed that the room suddenly seemed brighter again, although the ornamental lighthouse bulb remained dark. The light seemed to be coming from the metal base which held the light structure.

Gabe pointed to what appeared to be a small panel on the front of the base, and the light that was seeping through its edges. Kevin crouched down and pulled at the panel door with both hands. It came loose in his hands, and he fell backwards to the floor. The dropped panel door clanged loudly as it fell. The light went dark.

Kevin leaned over to look inside the open compartment. Inside there was a shelf about half way up, and sitting on it was a red velvet bag tied at the top. Kevin pulled out the bag and looked at the decorative embroidery on it. Both

Kevin and Gabe recognized the symbol—it was the Zeffner family crest.

Kevin reached in and pulled out the bag. He and Gabe could do nothing but stare at each other for what was actually seconds, but felt like an eternity. He untied the bag and emptied the contents into his hand. A clear, round, quartz-like stone that was about the size of a golf ball rolled in his palm.

"It's not glowing," Kevin said in a hushed voice.

"No," Gabe said. "But that's most certainly it. We have found the Tzohar."

Chapter Fifty Four

Stumbling through the darkness, the ascent from the basement to the top of the light tower had taken Gabe and Kevin over twenty minutes. The return trip took barely a quarter of that time.

As they descended the final flight of stairs leading to the basement, the flashlight which had been slowly dying since they entered the lighthouse, sputtered its last breath. They came to a sudden stop on the stairs as the darkness engulfed them.

"I can see the light from outside through the windows," Kevin said, pointing to the far basement wall. "I'm pretty sure that's where we came in."

Gabe and Kevin shuffled across the dark floor, slowly swinging their arms in front of them to avoid walking into anything. When they reached the place on the wall underneath the window, Kevin groped around and found some sturdy crates nearby. He stacked them below the window.

"Gravity helped us on the way in," he said. "But, we're going to need a boost getting out. I'll climb up first, then I can help pull you up if you need it."

Kevin was still clutching the Tzohar tightly in his hands. He slipped it into his inside jacket pocket, then zipped up his jacket to the neck. He climbed on top of the crates, then pulled the window fully open. Kevin put his upper arms on the window sill, and used only upper body strength to thrust his head and shoulders through the open window. He crawled on his belly, until finally only his feet were visible to the basement below.

After Kevin had stood up and stepped away from the window, Gabe followed his lead. He thrust himself up, and his shoulders caught on the window sill above. His legs flailed as he did so, and he heard the pile of crates crash below him to the floor. He put his head through the open window, and his arms pulled hard against the wooden frame.

"Hey, I thought the idea of you going first was so that you could help me," Gabe said.

Kevin said nothing in reply, but continued to stand just beyond the open window. Gabe continued to struggle, but eventually his torso cleared the open window.

"Well, if you're not going to help, you can at least get out of my way."

Gabe felt his legs clear the window, then he crawled to his knees. Brushing off his pants he stood fully upright.

He stared at the gun pointing directly as his face.

The same man they had run from in the museum, and who Kevin had said attacked him at Gabe's house, stood before them.

Noah Dew stared coldly at them, an angry snarl cast

across his face.

"The journey has ended," he said quietly. "I knew you two would lead me to where the old man had hidden the Holy Light."

"You fucking murderer!" Kevin yelled angrily. His voice was shrill and cut through the quiet night. At this point, he now was hoping that they would attract some attention.

"Rudy protected the Tzohar for years from worthless scum like you. You'll rot in Hell before you ever set eyes on it!"

"Rot in Hell," Noah Dew said slowly, fulling relishing the moment. A sick smile crossed his face. "Just like your old Nazi faggot."

Kevin lunged at the man, but Gabe held him back. Noah Dew cocked the gun and raised it closer to Kevin's head.

"I can take the Holy Light just as easily from your cold, dead hands."

"Wait!" Gabe exclaimed. He was in a near panic, and he realized that he had to somehow prolong this situation. Noah Dew stared at him. He seemed surprised by the outburst.

"But, we don't have the Tzohar!" Gabe said. "We found another clue—that's all. And, if it's like all the others, it won't make sense to anyone but Kevin and me."

Noah Dew stopped, and considered what was being said. He didn't believe the man, but he also knew he could not come this far, only to have the path end here.

"If you are lying to me, you will make your death so much more agonizing."

"I'm not lying," Gabe said, his heart pounding in his ears. "There was another clue, hidden in the light tower. It's right here…"

Gabe reached into the inside pocket of his jacket, and pulled out a small aerosol container he had purchased at the truck stop in Breezewood, PA. After their earlier experiences, he was afraid that it may prove necessary.

He sprayed the pepper spray directly into the man's eyes.

Noah Dew screamed in unbelievable pain, and dropped the gun as he struggled to raise his hands to his eyes. Later, Gabe would regret not grabbing the gun at that opportunity. But, the only thing he could think of at that moment was running as far and as fast as he could. Kevin had also realized that their opportunity for escape had arrived, and they both turned to run back toward their boat.

They reached the dock, and Gabe dived head first into the boat. Kevin pulled the mooring rope off the post on the dock, and gave the boat a shove into the water. He waited until it was almost too far away, then made a running jump from the dock into the boat.

The engine sputtered a few times before it finally turned over, and Kevin turned the boat into the dark lake and back toward the mainland.

Chapter Fifty Five

The small boat sped through the water at the maximum speed it could muster.

"Can't this thing go any faster?" Gabe asked. His voice struggling to rise over the sound of the boat engine.

"This is the best I can do," Kevin yelled in return. "I'm red-lining it the way it is now."

They had covered about two-thirds of the distance back to the mainline. Gabe could see the lights of Sandusky on the horizon in front of them. But, looking behind them, he could also see the search light of another boat, which seemed to be gaining on them—quickly. Obviously, their assailant had somehow found the strength to get beyond the pain of the pepper spray.

Gabe's thoughts were interrupted by sounds that no mechanical thing should ever make. The boat's engine clanged loudly, sputtered, then died completely. Smoke drifted from the engine, and the smell of hot metal filled the air.

"Fuck!" Kevin swore loudly. "We completely blew out the engine. We're dead in the water."

"I'm afraid that might soon be literal," Gabe said. "I'm pretty sure our friend from the lighthouse is coming up on us pretty quick."

Kevin looked backward toward the approaching boat.

"Ok," he said. "There's only one thing I can think to do. We'll kill all the lights on the boat and not make a sound. It's so dark out here, he could pass a hundred feet on either side of us and never see us."

Gabe knew the odds of Kevin's plan were not very good, but he honestly did not have anything better. They were alone, unarmed, and trapped in the middle of a dark lake with a known killer. It seemed hard to fathom that given the size of this lake, only they and Rudy's murderer were out here tonight.

Kevin powered down anything emitting a light source of any kind on the boat. Luckily, the motor had long stopped making any sounds that indicated life of any sort. Kevin put his finger to his lips, and he and Gabe crouched down into the hull of the boat.

In the silence that now enveloped them, they could clearly hear the sound of the other boat's engine. It seemed to grow louder by the moment. Then, the sound of the full throttled engine quieted, and only a hum continued.

"He knows we've stopped," Gabe whispered in the darkness. "He's slowing up to look for us." Even in the almost non-existent light, he could see the fear in Kevin's eyes, and knew it was only a mirror of what was in his own.

Gabe did not know how close the other boat was to them,

but from the sound of the idling engine he knew it was fairly close. He was hunched low in the boat, but he could see a spot light dancing across the water. First, it was far off to their right, then about fifty feet behind them; then, about thirty feet in front of them.

"He's sweeping his spotlight across the lake," Kevin said. "He's going to find us."

Gabe was startled at the eerily calm manner in which Kevin had described the inevitable. Both jumped when they heard the voice echo across the water.

"I know y'all are out there," the man said loudly. "I know y'all didn't just disappear, so why don't you just make it a little easier on yourselves and give me the Holy Light? Maybe then I won't make y'all suffer too much. Maybe."

Gabe shivered, both from the cold of the night on the open lake, and the sound of pure hatred in the man's voice. Just then, the spotlight shone fully on their boat, blinding him with it's brightness.

The other boat's engine suddenly revved up, as it began heading toward them.

"Time to play the only card we've got left," Kevin said.

He jumped up quickly, retrieving the Tzohar from this jacket pocket in one fluid motion.

"Don't come any closer, asshole!" Kevin yelled.

The man brought his boat to a dead stop about ten feet

away from them. He seemed unable to move his gaze from what Kevin held in his hands above his head.

"Yeah, that's right. I've got your fucking Holy Light. Although, it looks just like any other damn rock if you ask me."

Noah Dew made a sound that could best be described as a snarl. He pulled the gun from the back of his baggy pants, and pointed it toward Kevin.

"Stop right there, asshole. Or I'm tossing this fucking thing in the lake and you'll never find it. It will be gone *forever*." He stretched out the final word for dramatic emphasis.

Noah Dew was near panic. He could not come this close only to lose the Holy Light into the dark lake. He let out a primal scream that cut through the night like a knife, and he jumped into the air, easily crossing the open space in between their boats. He landed with a thud on the bow of their boat.

Kevin was startled, he had never expected the man to do that. Gabe ran to the far side of the boat, but that still put less than twenty feet between them. The man lunged for Kevin, and grabbed him by the throat.

"Gabe!" Kevin screamed, his voice cracking as he was choked. He threw the Tzohar through the air toward Gabe.

Gabe reached above his head, and felt the smooth stone land in his hand. He brought it down in front of him, and saw that the Tzohar had begun to glow.

Then, the world stopped.

Chapter Fifty Six

The world stopped.

The warmth of the light enveloped him. At that moment, he had never felt so safe or so secure. He stared into the light, and within it he could see all the answers. For one brief shining second he could understand everything—all of the secrets of the universe revealed themselves to him, as if from a familiar storybook he knew from his childhood.

He saw the full of his life—the beginning, the middle, and the end. But, the end did not frighten him, in fact he felt great comfort from it. In one flash, he saw every moment of his life—all those that had happened, and all those that would. The light emitting from the Tzohar was pure and boundless love. There was no other description for it.

"This is why I struggled so hard to protect it," he heard Rudy's voice in his mind. "This was the secret I knew, and how I always knew that once you loved someone, a part of you always would."

"Gabe…"

* * * *

"Gabe!" the voice shouted.

As quickly as the world had stopped, it began again. Gabe snapped back to his current reality. His experience had lasted only seconds, but it felt like a lifetime. His lifetime.

A third boat was racing toward them. Startled, Noah Dew released his grip on Kevin's throat, and he fell to the floor of the boat in a heap, gasping for breath.

"Gabe!" the voice yelled again through a megaphone from the approaching boat. It was Molly. She was one of several people in a Coast Guard boat that was closing in on them quickly. Gabe noticed that all were wearing dark jackets with FBI emblazoned on them.

The reality of the situation seemed to finally dawn on Noah Dew. He pointed his hand gun toward the Coast Guard craft and began firing. With rifles drawn, the other boat returned fire.

For a second, Gabe was frozen in place, unable to fully comprehend what was going on around him.

Kevin was laying on the floor of the boat covering his head. "Gabe, get down!" he shouted.

Gabe felt a sharp pain, then a burning sensation in his shoulder. He fell backwards from the boat into the cold, dark water.

For the second time that night, the world stopped.

Chapter Fifty Seven

COLUMBUS, OH-Three Weeks Later

Gabe switched on his computer as he enjoyed his third cup of coffee that morning. For some reason, since returning home his desire for coffee seemed almost insatiable.

He remembered very little after falling into the lake. He had awakened in a hospital room several hours later. Apparently, Kevin had helped pull him out of the water and kept him from drowning until those on the Coast Guard boat could fully pull him aboard. Nearly as soon as he regained consciousness, he realized that he no longer possessed the Tzohar.

His experience that night now felt vague, and somewhat disconnected. He could not remember the details of what he had seen in the light, but he remembered how it had *felt*. Every once in a while he would be reading, or walking through the grocery store, and he would be overcome with that feeling again.

He was only kept in the hospital for about a day. He had been hit by a bullet in the shoulder, but it was only a grazing wound. His more immediate health impediment had been hypothermia from the time he had spent in the water, but that too was easily rectified by simple medical care.

After being released, he and Kevin had been questioned extensively by the Sandusky Police, the FBI, the Columbus Police, the Dallas Police, and by the Mossad—which he had learned from his recent—and intimate—association, was the Israeli version of the CIA and FBI rolled into one.

They were interviewed separately and together, for what was often hours at a time. At several points in the interview process, Gabe had inquired as to the status of the Tzohar and its current whereabouts. In each instance, he was simply told that no such item was recovered, and that no proof of its existence had been discovered. Gabe and Kevin's comments on the Tzohar had been left out of all the official transcripts of the interviews.

Finally, though, all the agencies involved were satisfied enough with Gabe and Kevin's explanations of the events that they were released. Kevin had been taken to Cleveland where he would catch a return flight to Dallas; Gabe had been escorted home to Columbus. (Then, he had to figure out arrangements to retrieve his car from the Pittsburgh airport's long term parking facility.)

Noah Dew would not be able to tell them anything, or confirm or refute the existence of the Tzohar. He had been hit several times in the shoot out with the authorities, and had dived off the boat into the dark lake. He remained missing for several days, but his body was eventually found by some fisherman near one of the islands. The Ottawa County coroner concluded in his official report that Noah Dew had been shot twelve times. Any one of which would have been considered a fatal shot.

The official story was that Noah Dew had jumped into the lake to attempt an escape. Gabe, however, knew better. He knew that Noah Dew had dived into the water for one reason only—and that was to retrieve the Tzohar. Shot twelve times and quickly bleeding to death, the man's one last act was to try to finally hold in his own hands what he had called the *Holy Light*. A few days earlier, Gabe never would have been able to fathom such a thing. But now, after his own experience, he believed he could understand.

In one of the last interviews before being released, Gabe was meeting privately with Namir Yosef, the ranking official with the Mossad. They were nearly finished with the interview, when Yosef had reached over and turned off the recording device. He looked squarely into Gabe's eyes.

"You held the relic?" he asked.

"Yes," Gabe said, somewhat surprised by this sudden change in the stern Israeli's demeanor and tone. "I held the Tzohar."

"And, what was it like?"

"Life-altering," Gabe said quietly.

Namir Yosef nodded in understanding. "I've spent my

whole professional life in the service of protecting the relic, but I've never seen it with my own eyes."

"That must be hard," Gabe said, and Yosef raised a questioning eyebrow. "To dedicate your life to something you've never actually seen. It must be hard."

"Perhaps," Namir Yosef said softly. "But, isn't that the very definition of faith?"

Kevin was quickly determined not to be a person of interest in Rudy's murder, since there was very clear evidence—including DNA—linking Noah Dew to the break-in and killing. In addition to Rudy, Dew was also proven to have killed Peter Polasky, and JoAnn Tomson—the desk clerk at the motel in Breezewood.

As the FBI began to investigate Noah Dew further, they uncovered evidence of a home grown terrorist plot to bomb the Federal Reserve Banks, starting with the one in Atlanta. After all, nothing would shake the secular society more than destroying its financial system.

The Feds had enough evidence for a search warrant, and conducted a raid of the Millfield Valley Holiness Church compound, where they found stashes of weapons and even more details on the terrorist plot. Much of the evidence discovered by the Federal agents focused on the church's preoccupation with what they called the "money changers in the temple."

Nearly every adult member of the church was arrested, and the children placed into the foster care system. Nearly eighty years after its founding by Thomas Dew, the Millfield Valley Holiness Church simply ceased to exist.

The official line in the media was that Noah Dew had killed Rudolph Zeffner in an attempt to steal a valuable piece of art that the group would have sold on the black market as a means of financing the terrorist plot. The story was made even further marketable and romantic by the news that Dr. Zeffner had hidden the valuable artwork safely away to avoid such a thing ever happening. Many so-called experts speculated endlessly on air about what this valuable treasure must actually be, but Gabe was pleased to know that no one ever actually came remotely close to the truth. Due to their involvement, both Gabe and Kevin received numerous invitations to appear on everything from the *Today Show* to *Larry King*. Both refused every request.

Gabe knew that the plot concocted by Millfield Valley was far more dangerous than anyone could possibly realize. He had no idea exactly how they had planned to use the Tzohar, but he was sure harnessing its power somehow fit into their plans. He was relieved that it never went that far.

Together, he and Kevin had been able to fulfill part of Rudy's final wish—they had kept the Tzohar safe. Their only failure was that it was now lost again, and they had been unable to give it to the world as Rudy had wanted.

His thoughts were interrupted by the ringing of his cell phone. He looked at the caller ID. It was Molly Newman.

"Hey, how's my saviour-slash-hero?" he asked, answering the phone.

"Well, you know how it is," she answered coyly. "All in a day's work for a lesbian, you know."

"Yeah, I've heard that about your kind."

They both laughed, enjoying the casualness and easy camaraderie of the conversation.

"But, seriously. I really have to thank you for coming out on that boat and saving our asses. Speaking of that—how exactly did you know?"

"Well, I'm afraid I can't take credit for all of that," Molly said. "I was requested to join the investigation by the FBI, and the Columbus PD agreed to loan me out for a while. They were aware that we were friends, and thought you and Kevin might be less likely to bolt if you saw a friendly face. Speaking of which, you know you would have saved everyone a lot of trouble—yourself included—if you just would have turned yourself over to the FBI at the museum in DC."

"Yeah, maybe," Gabe said. "But when you think you're

wanted for a murder, the last people you want to see is the FBI. Not to mention, at that point we couldn't exactly tell the good guys from the bad guys. Plus, if we would have done that we never would have followed Rudy's path to the end."

"Captain Yosef from the Mossad was the one who knew you would be heading out to South Bass Island. He spoke to the curator at the Indian museum and was able to piece together the clues to come to the same conclusion you and Kevin did. Although, he was a little thrown by your last minute booking of a flight to Berlin. But, let's face it—you two weren't exactly difficult to track. One word of advice— don't give up your day job to become a spy."

"Well," Gabe said. "I'm glad someone figured it out. Otherwise they would have been fishing our dead bodies out of that lake instead of Noah Dew's."

Molly was silent for a moment, as if she was debating what to say next.

"So, are you going to talk to the media about what really happened?" she asked finally.

"Do you mean about the Tzohar? No—I don't really see the point. The FBI and even the Mossad ignored what we had to say, and they knew that it was the truth. Why would anyone else believe it? Besides, right now Kevin and I are considered heros for helping thwart a terrorist attack. When you talk to the media you can go from hero to crackpot in a heartbeat. Besides, enough people have died searching for the thing—I don't like the thought of promoting it to a new group of seekers."

Again, Molly was silent for a moment, but she was relieved at what Gabe had said.

"Well, don't think I just called to go on and on about you," Molly said, attempting to lighten the mood of the conversation. "I have some good news of my own."

"Oh, really?"

"Yeah, I'm actively pursuing a career change."

"What?" Gabe asked. "I thought you loved being a cop?"

"I do, but I'm setting my sights a little higher—I've been accepted to the FBI Academy."

"Molly—that's fantastic! What made you decide to do that?"

"Well, it's always been a dream of mine. And, after I helped them out by assisting to track down you two treasure hunting flamers, it seemed like a good time to work my new contacts."

"Well, I'm glad the treasure hunting flamers could be of assistance. When do you leave?"

"The next class session starts at the beginning of January. It's only twenty-two weeks, so I'll commute home on the weekends and Vickie will come out to Virginia to visit. After graduation I'll know where I'll be assigned and we'll figure out what to do about the house and everything from there."

"Well," Gabe said. "I'm absolutely thrilled for you. I really am."

"I know you are. And you know I love you right? Even if you are some silly queen who ignores my best advice when I give it to him."

"Yeah, I know. And, trust me the feeling is mutual."

✳ ✳ ✳ ✳

After hanging up with Molly, Gabe drank his fourth cup of coffee of the day. Again, he turned his attention back to his computer screen. He had not seemed to be able to make himself focus on work since he had been back.

He launched his e-mail, and saw that he had one hundred and seventy unread messages. He was double-clicking on the first one, when his phone rang again. Again, he looked at the caller ID before answering. It was Kevin.

"So," Gabe said answering the phone. "I was wondering if I was ever going to hear from you again. Use me to find some historical treasure, then just blow me off." he said, feigning mock hurt.

"Yeah, I'm sorry," Kevin replied, picking up on the joke. "I got back to Dallas and immediately had to start getting everything with Rudy's estate settled. I had a thought about what to do with his ashes, but I wanted to run it by you first. I'd like to send them to Mora Garza. What do you think of that?"

Gabe felt a tear well in his eye. "Kevin, I can't think of a better idea. I think Rudy would feel the same way."

"Well, good," Kevin said. "That's what I'll do. I also wanted to let you know that I have the condo in Turtle Creek for sale. I'm going out on the road with that show I told you about."

"Kevin—that's fantastic news. I'm so glad you decided to do that. Rudy would be so proud," he hesitated for a second, then added. "So am I."

"Well, it seemed stupid not to take the opportunity that I've always dreamed about. Steve and I..."

"Steve?"

"Yeah, Steve Quincy. He wrote the book for the show and we developed it together. We've been friends for a long time, but recently..."

"No need to go into any more details," Gabe said laughing. "Just please tell me that this isn't yet another May-December thing for you again."

"Are you kidding? I'm two years older than Steve."

Both laughed at the comment, and then silence filled in the gap after the laughter faded.

"Gabe, even though it was an unbelievably crazy situation, I'm so glad that you're the person that I experienced it with."

"Yeah," Gabe said. "Me too."

"Rudy always used to say that you know when you've really loved someone, because a part of you…"

"Because a part of you always loves them," Gabe said, finishing Kevin's sentence.

"Yes, and I think he was right."

"Kevin, I *know* he was right."

Again, Gabe felt the tears begin to well in his eyes.

"I also called to tell you to expect a package that should get there anytime now," Kevin said.

"A package?"

"Yeah, just a little something I put together to fulfill a promise. But, it's a surprise—you'll just have to wait until it gets there."

"Ok, ok," Gabe said. "I'll be patient. But, I expect some good seats when your show hits Columbus!"

"Don't worry. Front row, with backstage passes. We plan to open there in May."

"I'll be at every performance."

"I know you will. Gabe, take care of yourself, ok?"

✳ ✳ ✳ ✳

Gabe hung up the phone, and resumed looking at his e-mail. The first message was from yet another referral from Margo Hoffer who wanted to employ him to find some long lost item.

He heard his front door bell ring. Still a little jumpy after the recent experiences, he gently pulled back the door curtain to peer outside. He saw the familiar brown uniform of the delivery service.

He opened the door, smiling and greeting the young blonde woman delivering for UPS. He signed her electronic tablet, and took a box from her.

He put the box on the table in the foyer, and carefully tore the tape from the edges. He opened the box, and pulled out a wooden signboard about eighteen inches long and eight inches high, and a wrought iron apparatus clearly designed to hold and suspend the sign. He looked at the sign's etched lettering:

Lost Loves

Personal Treasure Recovery Services

He smiled to himself, and returned his focus to the box. In addition to the sign, the box contained a box of business cards and engraved business stationary. Both the business cards and stationary contained the same business name, with one added element:

Gabriel Patrick, Proprietor

On the top sheet of stationary, there was a handwritten note from Kevin.

Gabe—

I bet you thought I forgot about my promise to help you come up with a name for your business. I thought a lot about it, and it seems to me that "Lost Loves" best describes what you really do. Plus, considering our recent experiences, it seems especially appropriate. Anyway, I hope you like it.

Love,

Kevin

Gabe did like it. He liked it very much.

He smiled to himself, and headed back to his desk. He began responding to the e-mail from the new client who was searching for his very own *lost love*. It was time to get back to work, and he felt more motivated than he had in years.

Everything was going to be ok. *He* was going to be ok.

Then, he happily began the rest of his life.

Author's Notes

Sometimes when a work of fiction mixes with truth and historical legend, it can become difficult to know what is real (or, what is perceived to be real), and what has been created for the book. So, I wanted to take a few pages and sort out fiction from fact (or, at least, fiction from cultural legend).

To be completely honest, before I began the process of writing this novel, I had never heard of the Tzohar. In fact, this book began with an interest I had in the Archangel Gabriel. I was fascinated by the fact that despite all the mentions of angels throughout Christianity (and other religions, although Christianity was what I was most personally familiar with), only three were actually named in the Bible. As one of the named Angels (Michael and Raphael were the others), Gabriel played a major role in not only Christianity, but also Judaism and Islam. Islam even says that it was Gabriel who gave the Koran to Muhammad.

I knew that I wanted my novel to be in the genre of the historical "treasure hunt," in the tradition of Dan Brown, Steve Berry, and several of my other favorite authors. Unfortunately, while I had great interest in the legend of the Angel Gabriel, I was lacking the "treasure" for my hunt.

I first learned of the Tzohar while reading *The Archangel Gabriel in History and Tradition* by the theologian Roxana

Ileana Lavoschi (published by VDM Verlag Dr. Muller in 2008). This book described the Tzohar as a "glowing stone" and told the story of Abraham finding it in the cave. As soon as I read its description, I was pretty sure I had found the treasure that would serve as the subject of my book.

Some further research lead me to a few other excellent sources of information on the Tzohar. *Gabriel's Palace: Jewish Mystical Tales* (by Howard Schwartz) provided a very detailed account of the legend of the Tzohar, and provided most of its description in this novel. (The only part which was complete fiction on my part was the mention of the Tzohar in relationship to the early Mormon Church.) In addition, the website *Encyclopedia Mythica* (www.pantheon.org) provided a very good article on the Tzohar by the Rabbi Geoffrey W. Dennis.

After learning more about the legend of the Tzohar, I was amazed that it was so little known in contemporary society. Other than the more scholarly treatments by academics and theologians, there are very few mentions of the Tzohar in popular culture. One notable exception to that is *The Illumination*, a novel by Jill Gregory and Karen Tintori (2009, St. Martin's Press). While that novel tells a very different narrative than *Chasing the Light*, it's one of the very few works of fiction to feature the Tzohar. (Compare that to subjects like the Lost Ark of the Covenant or the treasure of the Templars, in which there are literally hundreds of fictional accounts.)

The locales of Dallas, Columbus, Washington, and Estepona are pretty accurately represented in their descriptions. I've spent quite a bit of time in the first three, and while I have only visited Estepona once, I hope I captured something of its charm and beauty.

The South Bass Island lighthouse description (and its current purpose) is based on truth. And, of course, the Museum of the American Indian is a real component of the Smithsonian, and the description of the building and its contents is for the most part accurate. However, its curator in this story is a product of the author's imagination.

Anyone who follows international news knows that the Mossad is the intelligence agency of Israel, and is one of the most secretive organizations in the world. However, the "bureau of special considerations" is pure fiction. (Well, at least as far as I know...)

The backstory of how Adolph Schmidt became a British citizen is based on the true story of the family of a woman I worked with several years ago in Dallas. Her father-in-law had been an Italian prisoner of war in England, and stayed on after the war with the British farm family with whom he had been assigned to work as a prisoner. I always thought it was a wonderful story, and I was always impressed with what it said about how there can be such a thin line between someone you call an enemy, and someone who you call a friend. When I was researching this book, I found that it was not that unusual of a circumstance—that as many as 25,000 prisoners of war chose to stay in England and make a new life after World War Two.

Doing the research for this book, one of the things that struck me most about the various legends of the Tzohar was how it reacted with different people in very different ways. What I found most intriguing was how it seemed to give each person exactly what he needed at the time. What Gabe really needed was to feel that everything would be ok; that his life was on track. So, that's what the Tzohar gave to him.

Sometimes, all any of us need is just to feel that everything will be ok.

Acknowledgements

Prior to this endeavor, I never understood when authors would say that "no one ever writes a book alone." However, that statement now makes complete sense to me.

First, I would like to think Scott, Jim, and Amit for being my three-man focus group, and giving me feedback (and encouragement) on the early drafts of this novel.

I also want to thank Dee Dee, my best friend of over thirty-five years. She and I have seen more movies and shows over the years than I can even begin to remember. At various points when I was writing this novel I kept thinking, "Dee Dee will like this part."

I also want to thank my parents, Ted and Isabelle Zarley, to whom this book is dedicated. My mother always told her children that there was nothing in the world they could not do if they wanted and tried hard enough. And, the amazing thing is—I think she always really believed that. She passed away a few weeks ago, and before that had been in a nursing home for over a year after a stroke and advancing Alzheimer's. Yet, only a few weeks before she died she asked me if I still like to write. Her natural instinct was always to encourage her children.

I credit any ability I have at all to tell a tale to my father— that man could tell a great story! And, while he's been gone for ten years now, there's not a day that I don't think about him, and remember one of his stories.

Along with my parents, I would like to thank my siblings, Thea and David. They both have always been exceedingly patient with their "baby brother," and have continually raised the bar for me to aspire to.

I would also like to thank many of the teachers of the Zanesville (Ohio) City Public School system. While never a top performing (or testing) district, my experience shows that dedicated, good teachers can always make a huge impact in the lives of their students. Over the years, I had some really excellent teachers, several of whom I'd like to acknowledge by name here: Linda Good, Robert Okey, Mark Burrier, Vicky Newman, Sue Holt, Ruth Sharrer, Jim McLaughlin, Peggy Rouch, Ken "Butch" Wilson, Judy Robinson, and especially Barbara Winsley-Stevens, who was taken from this world way too young.

Finally, I want to thank Scott. Who, for the past sixteen years, has truly been my partner—in every sense of the word. There's no way I ever would have attempted to write a novel without your love and encouragement, and I want you to know that I appreciate how you've always believed in me—no matter what. I think the Plain White T's can say it better than I ever could hope:

There's only
1 thing
2 do
3 words
4 you

About the Author

Joel Zarley wanted to be a writer since crafting his first story in the second grade. As a Journalism major at The Ohio State University, he followed an interest in business writing and communications and has spent his subsequent career in the area of corporate training and development.

He resides in Columbus with his partner and is currently working on his second novel, which will continue the treasure hunting adventures of Gabriel Patrick.

His website is www.purplepalmmedia.com.